AN INDISCRETION IN THE LIFE
OF AN HEIRESS

# An Indiscretion in the Life of an Heiress

BY

THOMAS HARDY

HARDY'S "LOST NOVEL"

Edited with Introduction and Notes

BY CARL J. WEBER

New York

RUSSELL & RUSSELL

1965

FIRST PUBLISHED IN 1935
REISSUED, 1965, BY RUSSELL & RUSSELL, INC.
BY ARRANGEMENT WITH CARL J. WEBER
L. C. CATALOG CARD NO: 65—13931

PRINTED IN THE UNITED STATES OF AMERICA

# PREFACE

This book attempts to rescue from oblivion a literary foundling thrown upon the mercy of the public in 1878 and never thereafter acknowledged by its father. The explanation of these fifty-seven years of neglect may now be surmised and further light thus thrown upon the development of a great novelist. The accompanying study of a " lost novel " is an attempt to suggest, not only why this foundling should, in spite of Hardy's neglect, be rescued, but also why it is deserving of careful critical attention.

The almost total inaccessibility of the original publication provides reason enough for this first American edition of the story. The original spelling and punctuation have been faithfully followed throughout.

The editor wishes to express here his grateful recognition of his indebtedness to Mr. Paul Lemperly of Lakewood, Ohio, for planting the seed from which the harvest of this book has sprung, to Dr. John C. French and Professor Raymond D. Havens of The Johns Hopkins University for helpful criticism of the manuscript, to the librarians of the Brooklyn Public Library and of Colby College for interlibrary-loan courtesies, and to his wife for that patient listening and helpful comment by which this study has been greatly improved.

C. J. W.

# TABLE OF CONTENTS

vii

# HARDY'S LOST NOVEL

Thomas Hardy died on January 11, 1928. Ten days later a special cablegram was sent from London to the New York *Times* resulting in a copyrighted article printed in the *Times* for Sunday, January 22. This article informed readers that "Thomas Hardy's first novel, entitled *The Poor Man and the Law*, was rejected by two publishers and then burned by the author, according to Sir Edmund Goose."

There were of course many Americans who recognized, in the *Times's* "Sir Edmund Goose," Hardy's life-long friend Gosse; but unless they later gained access to Gosse's article in the *London Times* for the same day, they had no way of knowing in what further respects the New York version differed from the London one. In the original disclosure by Sir Edmund Gosse, the title of Hardy's first novel was given as *The Poor Man and the Lady*; and London readers, instead of being told that the manuscript had been burned, were informed that Hardy had "destroyed, as he thought, the whole manuscript but lately he had come upon four or five pages of it."

Gosse made his statements on the basis of what Hardy himself had told Gosse in 1921. Hardy was then eighty-one years old. "This," wrote Sir Edmund, "or I am much mistaken, is anything but a small contribution. If I speak too confidently of the novelty of the

1

disclosure, I must be excused by the fact that so far as I can discover no other record exists."

But here Sir Edmund was wrong.[1] Another record did exist,—and one that did not depend upon the memory of an aged man. This earlier record, contemporary with the novel itself, had finally been printed, among the letters of Alexander Macmillan the publisher, eighteen years before Gosse's article appeared. Sir Edmund, in making his claim that no other than his own record existed, was not only ignoring the Macmillan account of Hardy's novel, but was continuing to deny it recognition, even when his (Gosse's) attention had been called to it. A note appended to his article in the London *Times* stated that Mr. George A. Macmillan had sent Gosse " a copy of the letter which his father, Mr. Alexander Macmillan, wrote to Hardy on August 10, 1868. . . . It is a very interesting document, supporting, but not superseding, what I have reported above." But Sir Edmund did not print the letter, nor did he disclose the fact that this detailed examination of Hardy's first novel was in print and had

[1] These words had been written and this study completed before I had read *An Enquiry into the Nature of Certain Nineteenth Century Pamphlets* by John Carter and Graham Pollard (London, 1934). It was with more than ordinary interest, therefore, that I came upon these words on page 36 of *An Enquiry*: " Gosse's story, so circumstantially set . . . , so convincingly garnished with characteristic details, must be wholly fictitious. His anonymous informant . . . is discredited."

been in print for nearly two decades. Had this letter been reprinted, or were it more accessible, Gosse's readers might have been better qualified to judge as to whether or not Macmillan's "superseded" Sir Edmund's own story.

Gosse was evidently not acquainted with the *Letters of Alexander Macmillan*, published in 1910, and the book is certainly not well known in America. I have found it impossible to pick up a copy during the past year, and even within a few months of its publication it was hard to find. I have seen a letter from Professor Joseph Warren Beach of the University of Minnesota, written February 8, 1912,—less than two years after the publication of the book. Professor Beach wrote: " I am much interested in the Alexander Macmillan letters of which you write; but unfortunately the volume is not to be had in Minneapolis libraries." There were doubtless few in America who both read Gosse's article and detected its inaccuracy.

We no longer have to rely solely upon these two records. For within a few months of the appearance of Sir Edmund Gosse's " disclosure," several other comments on Hardy's lost novel were offered to the public. Vere H. Collins provided an additional report in Hardy's own words; and in Mrs. Hardy's biography of her husband further comments by John Morley, by George Meredith, by Hardy himself, and by his wife,

3

were given. From six several sources, therefore, we receive a body of testimonials which enable us not only to go a long way towards reconstructing Hardy's lost story, but to correct errors and to bridge gaps in one or another of these records. The six authorities may, in the discussion which follows, be conveniently referred to by initials, thus:—

C : Vere H. Collins, *Talks with Thomas Hardy at Max Gate*; New York, Doubleday, Doran & Co., Inc., 1928; p. 54.
G : Edmund Gosse, "Thomas Hardy's Lost Novel"; London *Times*, January 22, 1928.
H : Florence Emily Hardy, *The Early Life of Thomas Hardy*; New York, The Macmillan Co., 1928; pp. 75-143.
Mc: Charles L. Graves, *The Life and Letters of Alexander Macmillan*; London, Macmillan & Co., 1910; pp. 288-292.
Me: George Meredith, in Mrs. Hardy's biography ("H," above).
Mo: John Morley, in Mrs. Hardy's biography.

When these reports are all gathered together, we find ourselves equipped with a surprisingly detailed knowledge of *The Poor Man and the Lady*. I will try to summarize this knowledge here, and in doing so will ask the reader to be patient while I itemize what we know. The inventory thus prepared in dull cataloguing fashion may lack stylistic grace, and the reader uninter-

4

ested in the logic of my argument may find the next few pages somewhat tedious. But for those who are willing to play detective with me, let me set our table of exhibits in order. Let me patiently piece together all the little bits of our jig-saw puzzle. Some come from one source, some from another. Let me re-arrange them in careful sequence, following the plot of the lost story from its beginning through to its tragic end; and then append, as a frame or border to our picture, whatever critical and bibliographical details we may find left on our hands. In order to avoid cluttering up the page with a lot of footnotes, I shall merely give (for those who may wish to go back to my authorities) the initial and page reference in each case. Then, after our cataloguing is all done, we can more expeditiously and intelligibly discuss the subject of this study.

Here, then, is what we know about Hardy's first attempt at novel-writing:—

1.—The title of the novel was *The Poor Man and the Lady.* (H, 75)
2.—The story was written "By the Poor Man"; that is, in the first person, as if it were an autobiography. (H, 75)
3.—The scene of the story was laid in Dorset and in London. (G)
4.—The time of the action was the nineteenth century. (G)
5.—The novel opened with pictures of Christmas Eve in a tranter's house. These were of good quality. (Mo, 77)

5

6.—The story included some admirable description of country life among working-men. (Mc)

7.—The country scenes, dealing with the " tranter," were the best in the book. (Mo, 113)

8.—The story chiefly concerned the son of peasants working on the estate of the local squire. (G)

9.—This Squire was the Hon. Fay Allamont. (Mc, 289)

10.—The hero was called Will Strong. (Mc)

11.—He showed unusual talent at school and was given a very good education. (G)

12.—The Squire had a beautiful daughter. (G)

13.—This daughter was known as the squire's " heiress." (G) The significance of this point will be disclosed later.

14.—Will Strong became an architect. (Mc)

15.—By accident he was thrown into the company of the squire's daughter. (G)

16.—Miss Allamont took a romantic interest in the young man. (G)

17.—Her parents, however, shortly forbade further meetings. (G)

18.—The two then corresponded, until the parents also forbade further exchange of letters. (G)

19.—Strong went up to London and there made a striking success. (G)

20.—He was introduced to the kept mistress of another architect. This Lady was a dancer at a music-hall. (H, 81)

21.—Exaggerated pictures of London life were given. These Macmillan called " essentially untrue." (Mc)

22.—The most important scenes were laid in London. (H, 82)

23.—Portions of the book described experiences or presented views in such effective language that, being written in the first person, they seemed to come directly from Hardy's own experience. Actually, they had no such foundation. (H, 81)

24.—Strong was awarded an architectural prize by the Palace of Hobbies Company. (Mc)

25.—This award was afterwards retracted in public. (Mc)

26.—The young man took up radical politics. (G)

27.—His views were those of a young man with a passion for reforming the world. (H, 81)

28.—There was a scene in Rotten Row, Hyde Park, which Macmillan thought was "full of power." (Mc)

29.—The Allamont family came up to London to their town-house. (G)

30.—Strong took to addressing public meetings. (G)

31.—He delivered a speech to working-men. (Mc)

32.—He spoke at a public meeting in Trafalgar Square. (G)

33.—He told the story of his own life in public. (Mc)

34.—Miss Allamont drove by him in her carriage. (G)

35.—Will Strong recognized her. (G)

36.—She stopped to hear him speak; her feelings were wounded by what she heard him say. (G)

37.—She broke off all relations with the hero. (G)

38.—Her London life introduced a number of ballroom scenes into the story. Hardy's report of ballroom conversation was heartless. (Mc)

39.—In writing these ballroom scenes Hardy drew on his own dancing experiences at Willis's Rooms in 1862. (H, 56)

40.—Miss Allamont went to a London concert. (G)

41.—Strong went to the same concert. (G)

42.—She sat in the last row of the expensive seats. (G)

43.—He sat quite near her, in the first row of the cheap seats. (G)

44.—They were both extremely moved by the emotion of the music. (G)

45.—She placed her hand on the back of her seat; he took it in his and held it. (G)

46.—They walked away from the concert together. (G)

47.—She asked him to call. (G)

48.—When he did so, Miss Allamont's mother happened to receive him. (G)

49.—The meeting was an unfortunate one: the mother fainted; her rouge ran down her face! (G)

50.—The Hon. Fay Allamont ordered Strong turned out of doors! (G)

51.—" Some scenes . . . read like some clever lad's dream." (Mo, 77)

52.—The Allamonts left London and returned to Dorset. (G)

53.—Strong also returned to Dorset. (G)

54.—He shortly heard that Miss Allamont was about to marry. (G)

55.—The gentleman (the Squire?) pursued his wife at midnight and struck her! This brought about a meeting of the lovers. (Mc)

56.—" The scene in the church at midnight has poetical qualities—but could it happen? " (Mc)

57.—The night before Miss Allamont's wedding, Strong went to the church. She came and met him there. (G)

58.—They had a very emotional interview. (G)

59.—It ended with a renewal of her avowal of love. (G)

Hardy told Gosse in 1921 that his novel " showed a

wonderful insight into female character. I don't know how that came about! " (G)

60.—The heiress decided to take things into her own hands, and in the course of events her life was endangered. (Mc)

61.—In the hope of saving his daughter's life the Squire sent for Will Strong. (Mc)

62.—Miss Allamont died. (Mc)

63.—The hero-architect offered the Squire, without charge, a plan for the daughter's tomb. (Mc)

64.—The Squire accepted Strong's offer, because it would cost him (the father) nothing. (Mc)

65.—" The story then ended, but Hardy could not recollect whether she married the proposed bridegroom or no. He racked his brain to remember, but in vain; he could not tell at all." (G)

The story, as supplied by Gosse, ends with No. 59 above. Hardy in 1921 " could not recollect " the ending (60-64 above) supplied by Macmillan's letter published in 1910.

66.—The story was loosely hung together. (Mo, 77)

67.—It was a sweeping dramatic satire of the squirearchy and London society and was " obviously pushed too far." (H, 81)

68.—Meredith strongly advised Hardy " not to nail his colors to the mast so definitely." (Me, 80)

69.—Much of the writing was strong and fresh. (Mo, 77)

70.—It impressed Macmillan as the work of a young man. (Mc)

71.—*The Poor Man and the Lady* was written too early for a successful socialist story. (H, 143)

72.—In literary style it presented the affected simplicity of

Defoe's, "which had long attracted Hardy . . . to imitation of it." (H, 81)

73.—Hardy wrote the story at Weymouth. (G)

74.—Hardy began the story in 1867 and worked on it until October. (H, 75)

75.—He finished copying his manuscript on June 9, 1868. (H, 76)

76.—He sent his manuscript to Macmillan on July 25, 1868. (H, 76)

77.—Macmillan wrote to Hardy on August 10, 1868. (Mc)

78.—Hardy received Macmillan's letter on August 12th. (H, 76)

79.—"Would you be willing to consider any suggestions?" (Mc)

80.—Meredith too thought that Hardy might rewrite the story, "softening it down considerably." (H, 82)

81.—This suggestion of a revision from both Macmillan and Meredith came with all the greater force to Hardy's mind, because literary criticism was not a field in which he felt at home. When John Morley recommended that he do book-reviews, Hardy thought to himself: "There is nothing in the world I could do less well." (G)

82.—Hardy carried the manuscript of his first novel away. (H, 82)

83.—He was conscious of the crudity and imperfection of the work. (G)

84.—Gosse stated that "there was nothing clearly known" about this first novel. (G)

85.—It has been stated that what he did with the manuscript is uncertain. (H, 83)

86.—"He could not remember," Mrs. Hardy reported. (H, 83)

87.—But on October 29, 1921 (the same year in which Gosse talked with Hardy about this lost novel), the novelist was very clear and definite about his manuscript. "When I was moving, I got rid of it." (C, 54)

88.—Gosse reported him as thinking that he had destroyed the whole manuscript. (G)

89.—Destruction of manuscripts was not Hardy's habit. "I generally publish everything." (C, 67)

90.—Macmillan, Meredith, and Morley "seem to have been the only ones whose eyes ever scanned the manuscript." (H, 83)

91.—Yet Hardy spent the autumn of 1868 rewriting some of the pages of his novel. (H, 78)

92.—He later fancied he may have sent it to some other publisher. (H, 83)

93.—"Spared by some accident," four or five pages were still in existence a short time before Hardy's death. (G)

94.—Hardy recalled the story definitely enough to be able to tell Gosse that these pages "were from the least interesting part." (G)

95.—Sir Sydney Cockerell, Hardy's literary executor, had this fragment bound, hoping that it might thus be preserved.

96.—Shortly before his death Hardy burned this fragment.

97.—As long ago as 1901 Hardy stated that his earliest novel "would never see the light." (G) Why?

98.—Gosse reports that Hardy was unable to believe "that the product of his unripe imagination would ever be likely to possess a historical interest," and that he

" deliberately put an end to a work which he had completed with great care." (G)

99.—Collins on the other hand got the idea that, whatever was done, it was not done " deliberately." He reports Hardy as saying: " It does not occur to authors when they are young, that some day their early unsuccessful efforts may come to have value." (C, 54)

In view of Hardy's well-known habits regarding the preservation of manuscripts, and of the reported revision of some of the pages of his novel in the autumn of 1868, and of his fancy that " he may have sent it to some other publisher," some further inquiry into the fate of this lost story seems logical; and if this inquiry is as successful as I think it may be, we may find ourselves able to understand exactly what Hardy meant when he said to Collins: " When I was moving I got rid of it."

To direct our inquiry I propose to add, to the inventory of our information given above, one further statement, Item No. 100, which does not refer to *The Poor Man and the Lady* but to another novel by Hardy. I cite our knowledge of the way in which Hardy treated the manuscript of a later work (*Tess*) in order to justify the hypothesis that his treatment of the manuscript of his first novel was analogous.

Item No. 100.—Hardy's first novel was not the only one which was rejected by publishers. Twenty-two years after *The Poor Man* was declined, he met with the

12

same experience with *Tess of the D'Urbervilles.* At that time he adopted a plan which Mrs. Hardy thought was unprecedented in the annals of fiction. He dismembered his novel.[2] One chapter was submitted here, another there; certain pages were kept at home. The remaining mutilated story was then submitted to a new editor. This treatment was a complete success. (H, 290-291)

It seems likely that Hardy thought of this plan of action and followed it in getting *Tess* into print, because he had tried it before; i. e., because he had already successfully done the same thing with *The Poor Man and the Lady.* There is one marked difference in the two cases. After *Tess* had been dismembered, Hardy put the original story together again and published it in 1891 in the form originally planned (though as recently as 1912 he discovered four pages,—cf. No. 93 above,—now inserted into chapter X, which had been inadvertently omitted when the reassembled novel first appeared). In the case of *The Poor Man* such later reassembling was impossible; for, instead of publishing the amputated chapters separately, Hardy had made use of them in other novels![3] The description of the

[2] For details, see Carl J. Weber, "On the Dismemberment of *Tess*," *Saturday Review of Literature* (11: 308), Nov. 24, 1934.

[3] For further illustration of Hardy's economy in creative work, see H. C. Webster, "Borrowings in *Tess of the D'Urbervilles*," *Modern Language Notes* (48: 459-462), Nov., 1933.

home of Squire Allamont was (I think) transferred by Hardy to *Desperate Remedies* (1871), where it is now found in Chapter V, ii, as a description of Knapwater House (based on the real Kingston House, near Stinsford and near Hardy's birthplace). The opening Christmas scenes in the tranter's house (see No. 6 above) went into *Under the Greenwood Tree* (1872), where they now make up the first eight chapters of that novel (H, 113). Some four or five pages were, like those from *Tess,* neglected and were finally burned (see Nos. 93 and 96 above). And the rest of the story, as rewritten in the autumn of 1868 (see No. 91), lay on Hardy's hands for ten years. In March, 1878, he and his wife terminated an idyllic two-years' residence at Sturminster Newton, and on the 20th of the month they moved to London (H, 156). What happened to the manuscript of the first novel? Did Hardy take it with him? "When I was moving I got rid of it." (C, 54). Three months later *The New Quarterly Magazine* (July, 1878) published " An Indiscretion in the Life of an Heiress "; and in this story we may read, I believe, the remainder of Hardy's first attempt at fiction.

In this literary dismemberment,—a permanent one as contrasted with the temporary mutilation of *Tess,*—I think we may find the explanation, not only of Hardy's declaration that *The Poor Man* " would never see the light," but also of the striking facts that *An Indis-*

*cretion* was never reprinted,[4] was never collected by Hardy, and that it has never yet been published in the United States. To the American public it is an unknown story.[5] When Yale University held its Memorial Exhibition of Hardy first-editions in April 1928, its catalogue of the exhibit made no mention of *An Indiscretion*. I know of only three copies of the *New Quarterly Magazine* for July 1878 in America. One is in the Library of Congress; one is in the Brooklyn Public Library, from which copy I have made my transcription; and the third is in the private possession of Mr. Paul Lemperly [6] of Lakewood, Ohio, to whom I am indebted for the idea of this study. It was his early acquaintance with this story of fifty-seven years ago that enabled him in 1910 to read Alexander Macmillan's criticism of Hardy's first novel with the eye of a detective; and for a quarter

[4] After these words had been written but before they were put into print, I was informed by Professor Richard L. Purdy of Yale University that Mrs. Hardy is about to have the story reprinted for private distribution. If this project is carried out, I shall have to add " by Hardy " to my statement above.

[5] That it is almost equally unknown in England is indicated by the fact that F. O. Saxelby's *Thomas Hardy Dictionary* (London, 1911) makes no mention whatever of either the characters or the places of *An Indiscretion*.

[6] Students of Thomas Hardy will recognize in this name the publisher of that interesting booklet *Jude the Obscure: A Letter and a Foreword* (privately printed, 1917), which presents the correspondence that passed between Hardy and Miss Jeannette L. Gilder in 1896, following her notorious review of *Jude* in the New York *World*.

of a century he has been quietly persuaded of the truth of the hypothesis, the soundness of which I am trying to demonstrate. Let me, then, proceed now to the evidence for believing that the story of 1878 incorporates a large part of the novel of 1868. The usefulness of my tedious itemization of our information about the lost novel will, I hope, become apparent.

In the list of one hundred items given above, the first sixty-four deal with the plot and the characters of the novel. Nine of these sixty-four points were adversely criticized by Macmillan,—his letter, we may assume, accounting for the disappearance in the revised story of items numbered 20, 21, 25, 33, 38, 39, 55, 63, and 64. Five additional items met with unfavorable comment from John Morley; hence the suppression of numbers 30, 32, 47, 50, and 51. Morley, for instance, objected to the scene in Trafalgar Square. In the revised story Trafalgar Square is gone, and we read of " Chevron Square " and " the Park." Three items (26, 27, and 31) disappear as the result of Meredith's advice, and the revised story when thus " softened down " is free from all socialism and politics. These eliminations involved the loss of three other items (22, 23, and 36), and one (perhaps 48) remained in manuscript until the twentieth century and was finally burned. Three others (5, 6, and 7) have gone into *Under the Greenwood Tree.* In all, this accounts for twenty-four of the

sixty-four items. We are thus left with a list of forty identifying features of the lost novel; and,—significantly,—*all forty are to be found* in the story of *An Indiscretion*!

In looking over the story published in 1878 with my inventory of *The Poor Man* in mind, one has no difficulty in detecting the signs of Hardy's revision. The title, *The Poor Man and the Lady,* has been discarded; but the story still treats of a poor man and a lady. In telling the story the use of the first person has been given up, but there is still the same suggestion of autobiography. The novel in 1868 about a prize-winning Dorset architect had been written by a prize-winning Dorset architect; and the story published in 1878 about a successful literary man was written by a novelist whose recent literary success had enabled him to exchange architecture for fiction. The setting of *The Poor Man* was Dorset and London, and the *Indiscretion* introduces no change. The time remains the nineteenth century. References to Wellington and Waterloo (see p. 54) indicate the date.

The characters, too, are essentially the same. The story still concerns the son of peasants working on the estate of the local squire; but, with the transfer of the parents to the pages of *Under the Greenwood Tree,* the hero is left with only a grandfather. The Hon. Fay Allamont reappears as Foy Allenville. *Foy* may be a

misprint [7] for *Fay*, and the change from *Allamont* to *Allenville* is thoroughly characteristic of Hardy.[8] Will Strong as a name disappears, but the hero of *An Indiscretion* is still a young man of strong will, and one (if the reader will forgive me) whose strength of character suggests main strength, and hence Mayne! At any rate, Egbert Mayne is the same poor man with a more romantic name! He still shows unusual talent and is given a superior education. He continues to walk in the footsteps of his creator: — that is, Hardy the architect described an architect; Hardy the novelist revised his hero into a young writer. The poor man retains his London success, and his architect's prize is replaced by literary fame. Miss Allamont reappears as Miss Geraldine Allenville, but otherwise the heiress remains unchanged. She is still the Lady; she is still the squire's heiress (see No. 13, p. 6 above); and "the Lady" of the first title is the "Heiress" of the second. Her mother disappears in the revised story, but the father continues to play the original role. Correspondence between the lovers and its prohibition remain unchanged.

The old plot is easily recognized under the new title. Accident continues in the story to play the part it played

[7] There are other misprints in the story; see footnote 6, p. 33.

[8] For further illustration of such a change, see Carl J. Weber, "The Manuscript Names of Hardy's Characters," *Review of English Studies* (10: 456-459), October, 1934.

in the novel. Two important London scenes are retained with only minor changes. In one of them Miss Allenville, while out driving in her carriage, passes the hero and is recognized by him. In the other the whole episode of the concert is retained, with only such changes as might improve the plausibility of the account of the end of that important evening. Similarly the plausibility of the scene in the Wessex church is improved,[9] thanks to Macmillan's criticism (see No. 56, p. 8); and midnight is replaced by dusk.[10] In *An Indiscretion* just as in *The Poor Man*, the lovers meet in the Dorset church [11] and the meeting has the same result. The heiress commits her indiscretion, and the story comes to a characteristically Hardian conclusion.

Hardy's first attempt at fiction was obviously intended to meet the usual Victorian three-volume requirement. It seems reasonably clear that the condemned contents

[9] For further illustration of Hardy's tendency to write the sensational and the unconvincing, see Carl J. Weber, "A Trip to Brazil," pp. 28-64 of *In Thomas Hardy's Workshop*, Colby College Monograph No. 6, Waterville (Maine), 1934.

[10] For further illustration of Hardy's interest in such minute changes, see Carl J. Weber, "Care and Carelessness in Hardy," *Modern Language Notes* (50: 41-43), January, 1935.

[11] Hardy's poem "A Poor Man and A Lady" (see *Collected Poems*, p. 752),—a poem which "was intended to preserve an episode in the story of *The Poor Man and the Lady*,"—suggests that originally the meeting was in a Mayfair (London) church. Line 33 reads: "We met in a Mayfair Church, alone." In revising the story Hardy wisely translated the couple back to Wessex.

of one volume were destroyed, the contents of a second found their way into other novels by Hardy; and that the contents of the third may be read, in a slightly revised form, in the story which is here presented for the first time to American readers.

CARL J. WEBER

COLBY COLLEGE
October 1, 1934

STINSFORD CHURCH

(The model for "Tollamore Church," in which the story begins. This illustration is reprinted from *In the Land of the D'Urbervilles*, copyright 1933 by Carl J. Weber.)

# AN INDISCRETION IN THE LIFE OF AN HEIRESS [1]

## PART I

### CHAPTER 1

When I would pray and think, I think and pray
To several subjects: heaven hath my empty words;
Whilst my invention, hearing not my tongue,
Anchors on Isabel. [2]

The congregation in Tollamore Church were singing the evening hymn, the people gently swaying backwards and forwards like trees in a soft breeze. The heads of the village children, who sat in the gallery, were inclined to one side as they uttered their shrill notes, their eyes listlessly tracing some crack in the old walls, or following the movement of a distant bough or bird, with features rapt almost to painfulness.

In front of the children stood a thoughtful young man, who was plainly enough the schoolmaster; and his gaze was fixed on a remote part of the aisle beneath him. When the singing was over, and all had sat down for the sermon, his eyes still remained in the same place. There was some excuse for their direction, for it was

[1] Reprinted from *The New Quarterly Magazine*, July, 1878. The original spelling and punctuation have been faithfully followed throughout.
[2] Quoted from Shakespeare's *Measure for Measure* (II, ii, 1-4).

in a straight line forwards; but their fixity was only to be explained by some object before them. This was a square pew, containing one solitary sitter. But that sitter was a young lady, and a very sweet lady was she.

Afternoon service in Tollamore parish was later than in many others in that neighbourhood; and as the darkness deepened during the progress of the sermon, the rector's pulpit-candles shone to the remotest nooks of the building, till at length they became the sole lights of the congregation. The lady was the single person besides the preacher whose face was turned westwards, the pew that she occupied being the only one in the church [3] in which the seat ran all around. She reclined in her corner, her bonnet and dark dress growing by degrees invisible, and at last only her upturned face could be discerned, a solitary white spot against the black surface of the wainscot. Over her head rose a vast marble monument, erected to the memory of her ancestors, male and female; for she was one of high standing in that parish. The design consisted of a winged skull and two cherubim, supporting a pair of tall Corinthian columns, between which spread a broad slab, containing the roll of ancient names, lineages, and deeds, and surmounted by a pediment, with the crest of the family at its apex.

[3] Probably sketched after Stinsford Church, where Hardy's heart is now buried. This church figures in many of Hardy's stories. See map, p. 85, and illustration facing p. 21.

As the youthful schoolmaster gazed, and all these details became dimmer, her face was modified in his fancy, till it seemed almost to resemble the carved marble skull immediately above her head. The thought was unpleasant enough to arouse him from his half-dreamy state, and he entered on rational considerations of what a vast gulf lay between that lady and himself, what a troublesome world it was to live in where such divisions could exist, and how painful was the evil when a man of his unequal history was possessed of a keen susceptibility.

Now a close observer, who should have happened to be near the large pew, might have noticed before the light got low that the interested gaze of the young man had been returned from time to time by the young lady,[4] although he, towards whom her glances were directed, did not perceive the fact. It would have been guessed that something in the past was common to both, notwithstanding their difference in social standing. What that was may be related in a few words.

One day in the previous week there had been some excitement in the parish on account of the introduction upon the farm of a steam threshing-machine for the first time, the date of these events being some thirty years

---

[4] A reminiscence of an event in the lives of Hardy's father and mother, described in his poem " A Church Romance." The Mellstock of the poem is the Tollamore of this story. See *Collected Poems*, p. 236.

ago. The machine had been hired by a farmer who was a relative of the schoolmaster's, and when it was set going all the people round about came to see it work. It was fixed in a corner of a field near the main road, and in the afternoon a passing carriage stopped outside the hedge. The steps were let down, and Miss Geraldine Allenville, the young woman whom we have seen sitting in the church pew, came through the gate of the field towards the engine. At that hour most of the villagers had been to the spot, had gratified their curiosity, and afterwards gone home again; so that there were only now left standing beside the engine the engine-man, the farmer, and the young schoolmaster, who had come like the rest. The labourers were at the other part of the machine, under the cornstack some distance off.

The girl looked with interest at the whizzing wheels, asked questions of the old farmer, and remained in conversation with him for some time, the schoolmaster standing a few paces distant, and looking more or less towards her. Suddenly the expression of his face changed to one of horror; he was by her side in a moment, and, seizing hold of her, he swung her round by the arm to a distance of several feet.

In speaking to the farmer she had inadvertently stepped backwards, and had drawn so near to the band which ran from the engine to the drum of the thresher

that in another moment her dress must have been caught, and she would have been whirled round the wheel as a mangled carcase. As soon as the meaning of the young man's act was understood by her she turned deadly pale and nearly fainted. When she was well enough to walk, the two men led her to the carriage, which had been standing outside the hedge all the time.

'You have saved me from a ghastly death!' the agitated girl murmured to the schoolmaster. 'Oh! I can never forget it!' and then she sank into the carriage and was driven away.

On account of this the schoolmaster had been invited to Tollamore House to explain the incident to the Squire, the young lady's only living parent. Mr. Allenville thanked her preserver, inquired the history of his late father, a painter of good family, but unfortunate and improvident; and finally told his visitor that, if he were fond of study, the library of the house was at his service. Geraldine herself had spoken very impulsively to the young man—almost, indeed, with imprudent warmth—and his tender interest in her during the church service was the result of the sympathy she had shown.

And thus did an emotion, which became this man's sole motive power through many following years, first arise and establish itself. Only once more did she lift

her eyes to where he sat, and it was when they all stood up before leaving. This time he noticed the glance. Her look of recognition led his feelings onward yet another stage. Admiration grew to be attachment; he even wished that he might own her, not exactly as a wife, but as a being superior to himself—in the sense in which a servant may be said to own a master. He would have cared to possess her in order to exhibit her glories to the world, and he scarcely even thought of her ever loving him.

There were two other stages in his course of love, but they were not reached until some time after today. The first was a change from this proud desire to a longing to cherish. The last stage, later still, was when her very defects became rallying-points for defence, when every one of his senses became special pleaders for her; and that not through blindness, but from a tender inability to do aught else than defend her against all the world.

## CHAPTER 2

She was active, stirring, all fire —
Could not rest, could not tire —
Never in all the world such an one!
And here was plenty to be done,
And she that could do it, great or small,
She was to do nothing at all.

Five mornings later the same young man was looking
out of the window of Tollamore village school in a
fixed and absent manner. The weather was exceptionally mild, though scarcely to the degree which would
have justified his airy situation at such a month of the
year. A hazy light spread through the air, the landscape on which his eyes were resting being enlivened
and lit up by the spirit of an unseen sun rather than by
its direct rays. Every sound could be heard for miles.
There was a great crowing of cocks, bleating of sheep,
and cawing of rooks, which proceeded from all points
of the compass, rising and falling as the origin of each
sound was near or far away. There were also audible
the voices of people in the village, interspersed with
hearty laughs, the bell of a distant flock of sheep, a
robin close at hand, vehicles in the neighbouring roads
and lanes. One of these latter noises grew gradually
more distinct, and proved itself to be rapidly nearing
the school. The listener blushed as he heard it.

' Suppose it should be! ' he said to himself.

He had said the same thing at every such noise that he had heard during the foregoing week, and had been mistaken in his hope. But this time a certain carriage did appear in answer to his expectation. He came from the window hastily; and in a minute a footman knocked and opened the school door.

'Miss Allenville wishes to speak to you, Mr. Mayne.'

The schoolmaster went to the porch—he was a very young man to be called a schoolmaster—his heart beating with excitement.

'Good morning,' she said, with a confident yet girlish smile. 'My father expects me to inquire into the school arrangements, and I wish to do so on my own account as well. May I come in?'

She entered as she spoke, telling the coachman to drive to the village on some errand, and call for her in half an hour.

Mayne could have wished that she had not been so thoroughly free from all apparent consciousness of the event of the previous week, of the fact that he was considerably more of a man than the small persons by whom the apartment was mainly filled, and that he was as nearly as possible at her own level in age, as wide in sympathies, and possibly more inflammable in heart. But he soon found that a sort of fear to entrust her voice with the subject of that link between them was what restrained her. When he had explained a few

details of routine she moved away from him round the school.

He turned and looked at her as she stood among the children. To his eyes her beauty was indescribable. Before he had met her he had scarcely believed that any woman in the world could be so lovely. The clear, deep eyes, full of all tender expressions; the fresh, subtly-curved cheek, changing its tones of red with the fluctuation of each thought; the ripe tint of her delicate mouth, and the indefinable line where lip met lip; the noble bend of her neck, the wavy lengths of her dark brown hair, the soft motions of her bosom when she breathed, the light fall of her little feet, the elegant contrivances of her attire, all struck him as something he had dreamed of and was not actually seeing. Geraldine Allenville was, in truth, very beautiful; she was a girl such as his eyes had never elsewhere beheld; and her presence here before his face kept up a sharp struggle of sweet and bitter within him.

He had thought at first that the flush on her face was caused by the fresh air of the morning; but, as it quickly changed to a lesser hue, it occurred to Mayne that it might after all have arisen from shyness at meeting him after her narrow escape. Be that as it might, their conversation, which at first consisted of bald sentences, divided by wide intervals of time, became more frequent, and at last continuous. He was pain-

29

fully soon convinced that her tongue would never have run so easily as it did had it not been that she thought him a person on whom she could vent her ideas without reflection or punctiliousness—a thought, perhaps, expressed to herself by such words as, ' I will say what I like to him, for he is only our schoolmaster.'

' And you have chosen to keep a school,' she went on, with a shade of mischievousness in her tone, looking at him as if she thought that, had she been a man capable of saving people's lives, she would have done something much better than teaching. She was so young as to habitually think thus of other person's courses.

' No,' he said, simply; ' I don't choose to keep a school in the sense you mean, choosing it from a host of pursuits, all equally possible.'

' How came you here, then? '

' I fear more by chance than by aim.'

' Then you are not very ambitious? '

' I have my ambitions, such as they are.'

' I thought so. Everybody has nowadays. But it is a better thing not to be too ambitious, *I* think.'

' If we value ease of mind, and take an economist's view of our term of life, it may be a better thing.'

Having been tempted, by his unexpectedly cultivated manner of speaking, to say more than she had meant to say, she found it embarrassing either to break off

or say more, and in her doubt she stooped to kiss a little girl.

'Although I spoke lightly of ambition,' she observed, without turning to him, 'and said that easy happiness was worth most, I could defend ambition very well, and in the only pleasant way.'

'And that way?'

'On the broad ground of the loveliness of any dream about future triumphs. In looking back there is a pleasure in contemplating a time when some attractive thing of the future appeared possible, even though it never came to pass.'

Mayne was puzzled to hear her talk in this tone of maturity. That such questions of success and failure should have occupied his own mind seemed natural, for they had been forced upon him by the difficulties he had encountered in his pursuit of a career. He was not just then aware how very unpractical the knowledge of this sage lady of seventeen really was; that it was merely caught up by intercommunication with people of culture and experience, who talked before her of their theories and beliefs until she insensibly acquired their tongue.

The carriage was heard coming up the road. Mayne gave her the list of the children, their ages, and other particulars which she had called for, and she turned to go out. Not a word had been said about the incident by

the threshing-machine, though each one could see that it was constantly in the other's thoughts. The roll of the wheels may or may not have reminded her of her position in relation to him. She said, bowing, and in a somewhat more distant tone; 'We shall all be glad to learn that our schoolmaster is so—nice; such a philosopher.' But, rather surprised at her own cruelty in uttering the latter words, she added one of the sweetest laughs that ever came from lips, and said, in gentlest tones, 'Good morning; I shall *always* remember what you did for me. Oh! it makes me sick to think of that moment. I came on purpose to thank you again, but I could not say it till now!'

Mayne's heart, which had felt the rebuff, came round to her with a rush; he could have almost forgiven her for physically wounding him if she had asked him in such a tone not to notice it. He watched her out of sight, thinking in rather a melancholy mood how time would absorb all her beauty,[5] as the growing distance between them absorbed her form. He then went in, and endeavoured to recall every word that he had said to her, troubling and racking his mind to the utmost of his ability about his imagined faults of manner. He remembered that he had used the indicative mood

[5] Mayne here thinks one of his author's most characteristic thoughts, for Hardy was ever ready to act on the famous invitation of King Richard II: "Let's talk of graves, of worms and epitaphs!"

instead of the proper subjective [6] in a certain phrase. He had given her to understand that an old idea he had made use of was his own, and so on through other particulars, each of which was an item of misery.

The place and the manner of her sitting were defined by the position of her chair, and by the books, maps, and prints scattered round it. Her 'I shall always remember,' he repeated to himself, aye, a hundred times; and though he knew the plain import of the words, he could not help toying with them, looking at them from all points, and investing them with extraordinary meanings.

[6] "Subjective" is evidently a misprint for "subjunctive," the magazine compositor reading " e " for Hardy's " un." The New English Dictionary gives no instance of the use of " subjective " as referring to the " mood " of the verb; and Hardy was certainly speaking, as does Sweet's *English Grammar* (I, 107), of " the distinction between indicative and subjunctive."

# CHAPTER 3

But what is this? I turn about
And find a trouble in thine eye.

Egbert Mayne, though at present filling the office of village schoolmaster, had been intended for a less narrow path. His position at this time was entirely owing to the death of his father in embarrassed circumstances two years before. Mr. Mayne had been a landscape and animal painter, and had settled in the village in early manhood, where he set about improving his prospects by marrying a small farmer's daughter. The son had been sent away from home at an early age to a good school, and had returned at seventeen to enter upon some professional life or other. But his father's health was at this time declining, and when the painter died, a year and a half later, nothing had been done for Egbert. He was now living with his maternal grandfather, Richard Broadford, the farmer, who was a tenant of Squire Allenville's. Egbert's ideas did not incline to painting, but he had ambitious notions of adopting a literary profession, or entering the Church, or doing something congenial to his tastes whenever he could set about it. But first it was necessary to read, mark, learn, and look around him; and, a master being temporarily required for the school until such time as it should be placed under Government inspection, he

stepped in and made use of the occupation as a stop-gap for a while.

He lived in his grandfather's farmhouse, walking backwards and forwards to the school every day, in order that the old man, who would otherwise be living quite alone, might have the benefit of his society during the long winter evenings. Egbert was much attached to his grandfather, and so, indeed, were all who knew him. The old farmer's amiable disposition and kindliness of heart, while they had hindered him from enriching himself one shilling during the course of a long and laborious life, had also kept him clear of every arrow of antagonism. The house in which he lived was the same that he had been born in, and was almost a part of himself. It had been built by his father's father; but on the dropping of the lives for which it was held, some twenty years earlier, it had lapsed to the Squire.

Richard Broadford was not, however, dispossessed: after his father's death the family had continued as before in the house and farm, but as yearly tenants. It was much to Broadford's delight, for his pain at the thought of parting from those old sticks and stones of his ancestors, before it had been known if the tenure could be continued, was real and great.

On the evening of the day on which Miss Allenville called at the school Egbert returned to the farmhouse as usual. He found his grandfather sitting with his

hands on his knees, and showing by his countenance that something had happened to disturb him greatly. Egbert looked at him inquiringly, and with some misgiving.

'I have got to go at last, Egbert,' he said, in a tone intended to be stoical, but far from it. 'He is my enemy after all.'

'Who?' said Mayne.

'The Squire. He's going to take seventy acres of neighbour Greenman's farm to enlarge the park; and Greenman's acreage is to be made up to him, and more, by throwing my farm in with his. Yes, that's what the Squire is going to have done. . . . Well, I thought to have died here; but 'tisn't to be.'

He looked as helpless as a child, for age had weakened him. Egbert endeavoured to cheer him a little, and vexed as the young man was, he thought there might yet be some means of tiding over this difficulty. 'Mr. Allenville wants seventy acres more in his park, does he?' he echoed mechanically. 'Why can't it be taken entirely out of Greenman's farm? His is big enough, Heaven knows; and your hundred acres might be left you in peace.'

'Well mayest say so! Oh, it is because he is tired of seeing old-fashioned farming like mine. He likes the young generation's system best, I suppose.'

'If I had only known this this afternoon,' Egbert said.

'You could have done nothing.'

'Perhaps not.' Egbert was, however, thinking that he would have mentioned the matter to his visitor, and told her such circumstances as would have enlisted her sympathies in the case.

'I thought it would come to this,' said old Richard, vehemently. 'The present Squire Allenville has never been any real friend to me. It was only through his wife that I have stayed here so long. If it hadn't been for her, we should have gone the very year that my poor father died, and the house fell into hand.[7] I wish we had now. You see, now she's dead, there's nobody to counteract him in his schemes; and I am to be swept away.'

They talked on thus, and by bed-time the old man was in better spirits. But the subject did not cease to occupy Egbert's mind, and that anxiously. Were the house and farm which his grandfather had occupied so long to be taken away, Egbert knew it would affect his life to a degree out of all proportion to the seriousness of the event. The transplanting of old people is like the transplanting of old trees; a twelvemonth usually sees them wither and die away.

The next day proved that his anticipations were likely to be correct, his grandfather being so disturbed

[7] "Fell into hand": i. e., the lease expired, and Squire Allenville regained direct control of the property.

that he could scarcely eat or drink. The remainder of the week passed in just the same way. Nothing now occupied Egbert's mind but a longing to see Miss Allenville. To see her would be bliss; to ask her if anything could be done by which his grandfather might retain the farm and premises would be nothing but duty. His hope of good results from the course was based on the knowledge that Allenville, cold and hard as he was, had some considerable affection for or pride in his daughter, and that thus she might influence him.

It was not likely that she would call at the school for a week or two at least, and Mayne therefore tried to meet with her elsewhere. One morning early he was returning from the remote hamlet of Hawksgate, on the further side of the parish,[8] and the nearest way to the school was across the park. He read as he walked, as was customary with him, though at present his thoughts wandered incessantly. The path took him through a shrubbery running close up to a remote wing of the mansion. Nobody seemed to be stirring in that quarter, till, turning an angle, he saw Geraldine's own graceful figure close at hand, robed in fur, and standing at ease outside an open French casement.

[8] Possibly suggested by the hamlet of West Stafford, on the further side of the river Frome from Stinsford, where Hardy's father owned property near West Stafford. See map, p. 85.

She was startled by his sudden appearance, but her face soon betrayed a sympathetic remembrance of him. Egbert scarcely knew whether to stop or to walk on, when, casting her eyes upon his book, she said, ' Don't let me interrupt your reading.'

' I am glad to have ——' he stammered, and for the moment could get no farther. His nervousness encouraged her to continue. 'What are you reading?' she said.

The book was, as may possibly be supposed by those who know the mood inspired by hopeless attachments, ' Childe Harold's Pilgrimage,' a poem which at that date had never been surpassed in congeniality to the minds of young persons [9] in the full fever of virulent love. He was rather reluctant to let her know this; but as the inquiry afforded him an opening for conversation he held out the book, and her eye glanced over the page.

' Oh thank you,' she said hastily, ' I ought not to have asked that — only I am interested always in books. Is your grandfather quite well, Mr. Mayne? I

[9] The first and second cantos of Byron's famous poem appeared in 1812; the last in 1818. Its success was so immediate that Byron was able to say: " I awoke one morning and found myself famous." Hardy again refers to this poem in his last novel, *Jude the Obscure* (1895). In his notebook Hardy recorded (on July 2, 1865) sitting up till 12.30 A. M. to read *Childe Harold*.

saw him yesterday, and thought he seemed to be not in such good health as usual.'

'His mind is disturbed,' said Egbert.

'Indeed, why is that?'

'It is on account of his having to leave the farm. He is old, and was born in that house.'

'Ah, yes, I have heard something of that,' she said with a slightly regretful look. 'Mr. Allenville has decided to enlarge the park. Born in the house was he?'

'Yes. His father built it. May I ask your opinion on the point, Miss Allenville? Don't you think it would be possible to enlarge the park without taking my grandfather's farm? Greenman has already five hundred acres.'

She was perplexed how to reply, and evading the question said, 'Your grandfather much wishes to stay?'

'He does, intensely—more than you can believe or think. But he will not ask to be let remain. I dread the effect of leaving upon him. If it were possible to contrive that he should not be turned out I should be grateful indeed.'

'I—I will do all I can that things may remain as they are,' she said with a deepened colour. 'In fact, I am almost certain that he will not have to go, since it is so painful to him,' she added in the sanguine tones of

a child. ' My father could not have known that his mind was so bent on staying.'

Here the conversation ended, and Egbert went on with a lightened heart. Whether his pleasure arose entirely from having done his grandfather a good turn, or from the mere sensation of having been near her, he himself could hardly have determined.

# Chapter 4

Oh, for my sake, do you with fortune chide,
The guilty goddess of my harmful deed
That did not better for my life provide.[10]

Now commenced a period during which Egbert Mayne's emotions burnt in a more unreasoning and wilder worship than at any other time in his life. The great condition of idealisation in love was present here, that of an association in which, through difference in rank, the petty human elements that enter so largely into life are kept entirely out of sight, and there is hardly awakened in the man's mind a thought that they appertain to her at all.

He deviated frequently from his daily track to the spot where the last meeting had been, till, on the fourth morning after, he saw her there again; but she let him pass that time with a bare recognition. Two days later the carriage drove down the lane to the village as he was walking away. When they met she told the coachman to stop.

'I am glad to tell you that your grandfather may be

---

[10] The thought expressed in this quotation (which I have been unable to identify) might have been presented by Hardy in a sonnet of his own composing. See his poem "Hap," written in 1866 (*Collected Poems*, p. 7), which concludes:
"These purblind Doomsters had as readily strown
Blisses about my pilgrimage as pain."

42

perfectly easy about the house and farm,' she said; as
if she took unfeigned pleasure in saying it. 'The question of altering the park is postponed indefinitely. I
have resisted it: I could do no less for one who did so
much for me.'

'Thank you very warmly,' said Egbert so earnestly,
that she blushed crimson as the carriage rolled away.

The spring drew on, and he saw and spoke with her
several times. In truth he walked abroad much more
than had been usual with him formerly, searching in all
directions for her form. Had she not been unreflecting
and impressionable—had not her life dragged on as
uneventfully as that of one in gaol, through her resid-
ing in a great house with no companion but an unde-
monstrative father; and, above all, had not Egbert been
a singularly engaging young man of that distracting
order of beauty which grows upon the feminine gazer
with every glance, this tender waylaying would have
made little difference to anybody. But such was not the
case. In return for Egbert's presence of mind at the
threshing she had done him a kindness, and the pleasure that she took in the act shed an added interest upon
the object of it. Thus, on both sides it had happened
that a deed of solicitude casually performed gave each
doer a sense of proprietorship in its recipient, and a
wish still further to establish that position by other
deeds of the same sort.

To still further kindle Geraldine's indiscreet interest in him, Egbert's devotion became perceptible ere long even to her inexperienced eyes; and it was like a new world to the young girl. At first she was almost frightened at the novelty of the thing. Then the fascination of the discovery caused her ready, receptive heart to palpitate in an ungovernable manner whenever he came near her. She was not quite in love herself, but she was so moved by the circumstance of her deliverer being in love, that she could think of nothing else. His appearing at odd places startled her; and yet she rather liked that kind of startling. Too often her eyes rested on his face; too often her thoughts surrounded his figure and dwelt on his conversation.

One day, when they met on a bridge, they did not part till after a long and interesting conversation on books, in which many opinions of Mayne's (crude and unformed enough, it must be owned) that happened to take her fancy, set her glowing with ardour to unfold her own.

After any such meeting as this, Egbert would go home and think for hours of her little remarks and movements. The day and minute of her accidental rencounter became registered in his mind with the indelibility of ink. Years afterwards he could recall at a moment's notice that he saw her at eleven o'clock on the third of April, a Sunday; at four on Tuesday, the

twelfth; at a quarter to six on Thursday the twenty-eighth; that on the ninth it rained at a quarter past two, when she was walking up the avenue; that on the seventeenth the grass was rather too wet for a lady's feet; and other calendrical and meteorological facts of no value whatever either to science or history.[11]

On a Tuesday evening, when they had had several conversations out of doors, and when a passionate liking for his society was creeping over the reckless though pure girl, slowly, insidiously, and surely, like ripeness over fruit, she further committed herself by coming alone to the school. A heavy rain [12] had threatened to fall all the afternoon, and just as she entered it began. School hours were at that moment over, but he waited a few moments before dismissing the children, to see if the storm would clear up. After looking round at the classes, and making sundry inquiries of the little ones

[11] Hardy himself was similarly interested in specific dates, and in his novels is at times definite enough in his statements to make it possible to work out a complete time-scheme for the action. For an illustration of this in the case of *Tess of the D'Urbervilles*, see Carl J. Weber, "A Careful Chronology," in *The Writer* (46: 236-237), Boston, July, 1934.

[12] In 1868 Hardy had been reading Virgil's *Aeneid*, "of which" (Mrs. Hardy informs us) "he never wearied." In this "heavy rain" with its results we may see an echo of the famous rain that influenced the lives of Aeneas and Dido. For further illustration of Hardy's classical borrowing, see Carl J. Weber, "Thomas Hardy's Aeschylean Phrase," *Classical Journal* (29: 533-535), April, 1934.

in the usual manner of ladies who patronise a school, she came up to him.

'I listened outside before I came in. It was a great pleasure to hear the voices—three classes reading at three paces.' She continued with a laugh: 'There was a rough treble voice bowling easily along, an ambling sweet voice earnest about fishes in the sea, and a shrill voice spelling out letter by letter. Then there was a shuffling of feet—then you sang. It seemed quite a little poem.'

'Yes,' Egbert said. 'But perhaps, like many poems, it was hard prose to the originators.'

She remained thinking, and Mayne looked out at the weather. Judging from the sky and wind that there was no likelihood of a change that night, he proceeded to let the children go. Miss Allenville assisted in wrapping up as many of them as possible in the old coats and other apparel which Egbert kept by him for the purpose. But she touched both clothes and children rather gingerly, and as if she did not much like the contact.

Egbert's sentiments towards her that evening were vehement and curious. Much as he loved her, his liking for the peasantry about him—his mother's ancestry—caused him sometimes a twinge of self-reproach for thinking of her so exclusively, and nearly forgetting his old acquaintance, neighbours, and his grand-

father's familiar friends, with their rough but honest ways. To further complicate his feelings to-night there was the sight, on the one hand, of the young lady with her warm rich dress and glowing future, and on the other of the weak little boys and girls—some only five years old, and none more than twelve, going off in their different directions in the pelting rain, some for a walk of more than two miles, with the certainty of being drenched to the skin, and with no change of clothes when they reached their home. He watched the rain spots thickening upon the faded frocks, worn-out tippets, yellow straw hats and bonnets, and coarse pinafores of his unprotected little flock as they walked down the path, and was thereby reminded of the hopelessness of his attachment, by perceiving how much more nearly akin was his lot to theirs than to hers.

Miss Allenville, too, was looking at the children, and unfortunately she chanced to say, as they toddled off, ' Poor little wretches! '

A sort of despairing irritation at her remoteness from his plane, as implied by her pitying the children so unmercifully impelled him to remark, ' Say poor little *children,* madam.'

She was silent—awkwardly silent.

' I suppose I must walk home,' she said, when about half a minute had passed. ' Nobody knows where I am, and the carriage may not find me for hours.'

' I'll go for the carriage,' said Egbert readily.

But he did not move. While she had been speaking, there had grown up in him a conviction that these opportunities of seeing her would soon necessarily cease. She would get older, and would perceive the incorrectness of being on intimate terms with him merely because he had snatched her from danger. He would have to engage in a more active career, and go away. Such ideas brought on an irresistible climax to an intense and long-felt desire. He had just reached that point in the action of passion upon mind at which it masters judgment.

It was almost dark in the room, by reason of the heavy clouds and nearness of the night. But the fire had just flamed up brightly in the grate, and it threw her face and form into ruddy relief against the gray wall behind.

Suddenly rushing towards her, he seized her hand before she comprehended his intention, kissed it tenderly, and clasped her in his arms. Her soft body yielded like wool under his embrace. As suddenly releasing her he turned, and went back to the other end of the room.

Egbert's feeling as he retired was that he had committed a crime. The madness of the action was apparent to him almost before it was completed. There seemed not a single thing left for him to do, but to go

into life-long banishment for such sacrilege. He faced round and regarded her. Her features were not visible enough to judge of their expression. All that he could discern through the dimness and his own agitation was that for some time she remained quite motionless. Her state was probably one of suspension; as with Ulysses before Melanthus, she may have—

Entertained a breast
That in the strife of all extremes did rest.[18]

In one, two, or five minutes—neither of them ever knew exactly how long—apparently without the motion of a limb, she glided noiselessly to the door and vanished.

Egbert leant himself against the wall, almost distracted. He could see absolutely no limit to the harm that he had done by his wild and unreasoning folly. 'Am I a man to thus ill-treat the loveliest girl that ever was born? Sweet injured creature—how she will hate me!' These were some of the expressions that he murmured in the twilight of that lonely room.

Then he said that she certainly had encouraged him, which, unfortunately for her, was only too true. She had seen that he was always in search of her, and she

[18] Quoted from an unidentified translation of the Odyssey, XVII. Hardy retained his interest in the Greek epic for many years, and twenty years later recorded another Homeric echo in chapter 43 of *Tess*.

49

did not put herself out of his way. He was sure that she liked him to admire her. 'Yet, no,' he murmured, 'I will not excuse myself at all.'

The night passed away miserably. One conviction by degrees overruled all the rest in his mind—that if she knew precisely how pure had been his longing towards her, she could not think badly of him. His reflections resulted in a resolve to get an interview with her, and make his defence and explanation in full. The decision come to, his impatience could scarcely preserve him from rushing to Tollamore House that very daybreak, and trying to get into her presence, though it was the likeliest of suppositions that she would never see him.

Every spare minute of the following days he hovered round the house, in hope of getting a glimpse of her; but not once did she make herself visible. He delayed taking the extreme step of calling, till the hour came when he could delay no longer. On a certain day he rang the bell with a mild air, and disguised his feelings by looking as if he wished to speak to her merely on copy-books, slates, and other school matters, the school being professedly her hobby. He was told that Miss Allenville had gone on a visit to some relatives thirty-five miles off, and that she would probably not return for a month.

As there was no help for it, Egbert settled down to wait as he best could, not without many misgivings lest

his rash action, which a prompt explanation might have toned down and excused, would now be the cause of a total estrangement between them, so that nothing would restore him to the place he had formerly held in her estimation. That she had ever seriously loved him he did not hope or dream; but it was intense pain to him to be out of her favour.

## Chapter 5

So I soberly laid my last plan
To extinguish the man.
Round his creep-hole, with never a break,
Ran my fires for his sake;
Over-head did my thunder combine
With my underground mine:
Till I looked from my labour content
To enjoy the event.
When sudden—how think ye the end? [14]

A week after the crisis mentioned above, it was secretly whispered to Egbert's grandfather that the park enlargement scheme was after all to be proceeded with; that Miss Allenville was extremely anxious to have it put in hand as soon as possible. Farmer Broadford's farm was to be added to Greenman's, as originally intended, and the old house that Broadford lived in was to be pulled down as an encumbrance.

'It is she this time!' murmured Egbert, gloomily. 'Then I did offend her, and mortify her; and she is resentful.'

The excitement of his grandfather again caused him much alarm, and even remorse. Such was the responsiveness of the farmer's physical to his mental state

[14] Quoted from Browning's *Instans Tyrannus*, 53-61. During the 1880's Hardy met Browning frequently in London. His interest in the poems of the elder poet lasted throughout his life. The night before Hardy died he asked to have one of Browning's poems read to him. See also note 19 (p. 75).

that in the course of a week his usual health failed, and his gloominess of mind was followed by dimness of sight and giddiness. By much persuasion Egbert induced him to stay at home for a day or two; but indoors he was the most restless of creatures, through not being able to engage in the pursuits to which he had been accustomed from his boyhood. He walked up and down, looking wistfully out of the window, shifting the positions of books and chairs, and putting them back again, opening his desk and shutting it after a vacant look at the papers, saying he should never get settled in another farm at his time of life, and evincing all the symptoms of nervousness and excitability.

Meanwhile Egbert anxiously awaited Miss Allenville's return, more resolved than ever to obtain audience of her, and beg her not to visit upon an unoffending old man the consequences of a young one's folly. Any retaliation upon himself he would accept willingly, and own to be well deserved.

At length, by making off-hand inquiries (for he dared not ask directly for her again) he learnt that she was to be at home on the Thursday. The following Friday and Saturday he kept a sharp lookout; and, when lingering in the park for at least the tenth time in that half-week, a sudden rise in the ground revealed her coming along the path.

Egbert stayed his advance, in order that, if she really

objected to see him, she might easily strike off into a side path or turn back.

She did not accept the alternatives, but came straight on to where he lingered, averting her face waywardly as she approached. When she was within a few steps of him he could see that the trimmings of her dress trembled like leaves. He cleared his dry throat to speak.

' Miss Allenville,' he said, humbly taking off his hat, ' I should be glad to say one word to you, if I may.'

She looked at him for just one moment, but said nothing; and he could see that the expression of her face was flushed, and her mood skittish. The place they were standing in was a remote nook, hidden by the trunks and boughs, so that he could afford to give her plenty of time, for there was no fear of their being observed or overheard. Indeed, knowing that she often walked that way, Egbert had previously surveyed the spot and thought it suitable for the occasion, much as Wellington antecedently surveyed the field of Waterloo.[15]

Here the young man began his pleading speech to her. He dilated upon his sensations when first he saw her; and as he became warmed by his oratory he spoke of all his inmost perturbations on her account without the slightest reserve. He related with much natural

[15] This reference to the famous battle of 1815 helps to date the action. See notes 9 (p. 39) and 11 (p. 45).

eloquence how he had tried over and over again not to love her, and how he had loved her in spite of that trying; of his intention never to reveal his passion, till their situation on that rainy evening prompted the impulse which ended in that irreverent action of his; and earnestly asked her to forgive him—not for his feelings, since they were his own to command or blame—but for the way in which he testified of them to one so cultivated and so beautiful.

Egbert was flushed and excited by the time that he reached this point in his tale.

Her eyes were fixed on the grass; and then a tear stole quietly from its corner, and wandered down her cheek. She tried to say something, but her usually adroit tongue was unequal to the task. Ultimately she glanced at him, and murmured, ' I forgive you '; but so inaudibly, that he only recognized the words by their shape upon her lips.

She looked not much more than a child now, and Egbert thought with sadness that her tear and her words were perhaps but the result, the one of a transitory sympathy, the other of a desire to escape. They stood silent for some seconds, and the dressing-bell of the house began ringing. Turning slowly away without another word she hastened out of his sight.

When Egbert reached home some of his grandfather's old friends were gathered there, sympathising

with him on the removal he would have to submit to if report spoke truly. Their sympathy was rather more for him to bear than their indifference; and as Egbert looked at the old man's bent figure, and at the expression of his face, denoting a wish to sink under the earth, out of sight and out of trouble, he was greatly depressed, and he said inwardly, 'What a fool I was to ask forgiveness of a woman who can torture my only relative like this! Why do I feel her to be glorious? Oh that I had never seen her!'

The next day was Sunday, and his grandfather being too unwell to go out, Egbert went to the evening service alone. When it was over, the rector detained him in the churchyard to say a few words about the next week's undertakings. This was soon done, and Egbert turned back to leave the now empty churchyard. Passing the porch he saw Miss Allenville coming out of the door.

Egbert said nothing, for he knew not what to say; but she spoke. 'Ah, Mr. Mayne, how beautiful the west sky looks! It is the finest sunset we have had this spring.'

'It is very beautiful,' he replied, without looking westward a single degree. 'Miss Allenville,' he said reproachfully, 'you might just have thought whether, for the sake of reaching one guilty person, it was worth while to deeply wound an old man.'

' I do not allow you to say that,' she answered with proud quickness. ' Still, I will listen just this once.'

' Are you glad you asserted your superiority to me by putting in motion again that scheme for turning him out? '

' I merely left off hindering it,' she said.

'Well, we shall go now,' continued Egbert, ' and make room for newer people. I hope you forgive what caused it all.'

' You talk in that strain to make me feel regrets; and you think that because you are read in a few books you may say or do anything.'

' No, no. That's unfair.'

' I will try to alter it—that your grandfather may not leave. Say that you forgive me for thinking he and yourself had better leave—as I forgive you for what you did. But remember, nothing of that sort ever again.'

' Forgive you? Oh, Miss Allenville! ' said he in a wild whisper, ' I wish you had sinned a hundred times as much, that I might show how readily I can forgive all.'

She had looked as if she would have held out her hand; but, for some reason or other, directly he had spoken with emotion it was not so well for him as when he had spoken to wound her. She passed on silently, and entered the private gate to the house.

A day or two after this, about three o'clock in the

afternoon, and whilst Egbert was giving a lesson in geography, a lad burst into the school with the tidings that Farmer Broadford had fallen from a corn-stack they were threshing, and hurt himself severely.

The boy had borrowed a horse to come with, and Mayne at once made him gallop off with it for a doctor. Dismissing the children, the young man ran home full of forebodings. He found his relative in a chair, held up by two of his labouringmen. He was put to bed, and seeing how pale he was, Egbert gave him a little wine, and bathed the parts which had been bruised by the fall.

Egbert had at first been the more troubled at the event through believing that his grandfather's fall was the result of his low spirits and mental uneasiness; and he blamed himself for letting so infirm a man go out upon the farm till quite recovered. But it turned out that the actual cause of the accident was the breaking of the ladder that he had been standing on. When the surgeon had seen him he said that the external bruises were mere trifles; but that the shock had been great, and had produced internal injuries highly dangerous to a man in that stage of life.

His grandson was of opinion in later years that the fall only hastened by a few months a dissolution which would soon have taken place under any circumstances, from the natural decay of the old man's constitution.

His pulse grew feeble and his voice weak, but he continued in a comparatively firm state of mind for some days, during which he talked to Egbert a great deal.

Egbert trusted that the illness would soon pass away; his anxiety for his grandfather was great. When he was gone not one of the family would be left but himself. But in spite of hope the younger man perceived that death was really at hand. And now arose a question. It was certainly a time to make confidences, if they were ever to be made; should he, then, tell his grandfather, who knew the Allenvilles so well, of his love for Geraldine? At one moment it seemed duty; at another it seemed a graceful act, to say the least.

Yet Egbert might never have uttered a word but for a remark of his grandfather's which led up to the very point. He was speaking of the farm and of the Squire, and thence he went on to the daughter.

'She, too,' he said, 'seems to have that reckless spirit which was in her mother's family, and ruined her mother's father at the gaming table, though she's too young to show much of it yet.'

'I hope not,' said Egbert fervently.

'Why? What be the Allenvilles to you—not that I wish the girl harm?'

'I think that she is the very best thing in the world. I—love her deeply.'

His grandfather's eyes were set on the wall. 'Well,

well, my poor boy,' came softly from his mouth. ' What
made ye think of loving her? Ye may as well love a
mountain, for any return you'll ever get. Do she know
of it?'

' She guesses it. It was my saving her from the
threshing-machine that began it.'

' And she checks you?'

' Well—no.'

' Egbert,' he said after a silence, ' I am grieved, for it
can but end in pain. Mind, she's an inexperienced girl.
She never thinks of what trouble she may get herself
into with her father and with her friends. And mind
this, my lad, as another reason for dropping it; however
honourable your love may be, you'll never get credit
for your honour. Nothing you can do will ever root
out the notion of people that where the man is poor
and the woman is high-born he's a scamp and she's an
angel.'

' She's very good.'

' She's thoughtless, or she'd never encourage you.
You must try not to see her.'

' I will never put myself in her way again.'

The subject was mentioned no more then. The next
day the worn-out old farmer died, and his last request
to Egbert was that he would do nothing to tempt
Geraldine Allenville to think of him further.

# CHAPTER 6

Hath misery made thee blind
To the fond workings of a woman's mind?
And must I say—albeit my heart rebel
With all that woman feels but should not tell;
Because despite thy faults, that heart is moved—
It feared thee, thank'd thee, pitied, madden'd, loved?

It was in the evening of the day after Farmer Broad-ford's death that Egbert first sat down in the house alone. The bandy-legged little man who had acted as his grandfather's groom of the chambers and stables simultaneously had gone into the village. The candles were not yet lighted, and Mayne abstractedly watched upon the pale wall the latter rays of sunset slowly changing into the white shine of a moon a few days old. The ancient family clock had stopped for want of winding, and the intense silence that prevailed seemed more like the bodily presence of some quality than the mere absence of sound.

He was thinking how many were the indifferent expressions which he had used towards the poor body lying cold upstairs — the only relation that he had latterly had upon earth — which might as well have been left unsaid; of how far he had been from practically attempting to do what in theory he called best — to make the most of every pulse of natural affection; that he had never heeded or particularly inquired the

61

meaning of the different pieces of advice which the kind old man had tendered from time to time; that he had never even thought of asking for any details of his grandfather's history.

His musings turned upon Geraldine. He had promised to seek her no more, and he would keep his promise. Her interest in him might only be that of an exceedingly romantic and freakish soul, awakened but through 'lack of other idleness,' and because sound sense suggested to her that it was a thing dangerous to do; for it seemed that she was ever and only moved by the superior of two antagonistic forces. She had as yet seen little or no society, she was only seventeen; and hence it was possible that a week of the town and fashion into which she would soon be initiated might blot out his very existence from her memory.

He was sitting with his back to the window, meditating in this minor key, when a shadow darkened the opposite moonlit wall. Egbert started. There was a gentle tap at the door; and he opened it to behold the well-known form of the lady in his mind.

'Mr. Mayne, are you alone?' she whispered, full of agitation.

'Quite alone, excepting my poor grandfather's body upstairs,' he answered, as agitated as she.

Then out it all came. 'I couldn't help coming — I hope — oh, I do so pray — that it was not through me that he died. Was it I, indeed, who killed him?

They say it was the effect of the news that he was to leave the farm. I would have done anything to hinder his being turned out had I only reflected! And now he is dead. It was so cruel to an old man like him; and now you have nobody in the world to care for you, have you, Egbert — except me?'

The ice was wholly broken. He took her hand in both his own and began to assure her that her alarm was grounded on nothing whatever. And yet he was almost reluctant to assure her out of so sweet a state. And when he had said over and over again that his grandfather's fall had nothing to do with his mental condition, that the utmost result of her hasty proceeding was a sadness of spirit in him, she still persisted, as is the custom of women, in holding to that most painful possibility as the most likely, simply because it wounded her most. It was a long while before she would be convinced of her own innocence, but he maintained it firmly, and she finally believed.

They sat down together, restraint having quite died out between them. The fine-lady portion of her existence, of which there was never much, was in abeyance, and they spoke and acted simply as a young man and woman who were beset by common troubles, and who had like hopes and fears.

'And you will never blame me again for what I did?' said Egbert.

'I never blamed you much,' she murmured with arch

simplicity. 'Why should it be wrong for me to be honest with you now, and tell everything you want to know?'

Mayne was silent. That was a difficult question for a conscientious man to answer. Here was he nearly twenty-one years of age, and with some experience of life, while she was a girl nursed up like an exotic, with no real experience, and but little over seventeen — though from the fineness of her figure she looked more womanly than she really was. It plainly had not crossed her young mind that she was on the verge of committing the most horrible social sin — that of loving beneath her, and owning that she so loved. Two years thence she might see the imprudence of her conduct, and blame him for having led her on. Ought he not then, considering his grandfather's words, to say that it was wrong for her to be honest; that she should forget him, and fix her mind on matters appertaining to her order? He could not do it—he let her drift sweetly on.

'I think more of you than anybody in the whole world,' he replied. 'And you will allow me to, will you not? — let me always keep you in my heart, and almost worship you?'

'That would be wrong. But you may think of me, if you like to, very much; it will give me great pleasure. I don't think my father thinks of me at all — or anybody, except you. I said the other day I would never think of you again, but I have done it, a good many

times. It is all through being obliged to care for somebody whether you will or no.'

' And you will go on thinking of me? '

' I will do anything to — oblige you.'

Egbert, on the impulse of the moment, bent over her and raised her little hand to his lips. He reverenced her too much to think of kissing her cheek. She knew this, and was thrilled through with the delight of being adored as one from above the sky.

Up to this day of its existence their affection had been a battle, a species of antagonism wherein his heart and the girl's had faced each other, and being anxious to do honour to their respective parts. But now it was a truce and a settlement, in which each one took up the other's utmost weakness, and was careless of concealing his and her own.

Surely, sitting there as they sat then, a more unreasoning condition of mind as to how this unequal conjunction would end never existed. They swam along through the passing moments, not a thought of duty on either side, not a further thought on his but that she was the dayspring of his life, that he would die for her a hundred times; superadded to which was a shapeless uneasiness that she would in some manner slip away from him. The solemnity of the event that had just happened would have shown up to him any ungenerous feeling in strong colours — and he had reason afterwards to examine the epoch narrowly; but it only

seemed to demonstrate how instinctive and uncalculating was the love that worked within him.

It was almost time for her to leave. She held up her watch to the moonlight. Five minutes more she would stay; then three minutes, and no longer. 'Now I'm going,' she said. 'Do you forgive me entirely?'

'How shall I say "Yes" without assuming that there was something to forgive?'

'Say "Yes." It is sweeter to fancy I am forgiven than to think I have not sinned.'

With this she went to the door. Egbert accompanied her through the wood, and across a portion of the park, till they were about a hundred yards from the house, when he was forced to bid her farewell.

The old man was buried on the following Sunday. During several weeks afterwards Egbert's sole consolation under his loss was in thinking of Geraldine, for they did not meet in private again till some time had elapsed. The ultimate issue of this absorption in her did not concern him at all: it seemed to be in keeping with the system of his existence now that he should have an utterly inscrutable to-morrow.

## Chapter 7

Come forward, some great marshall, and organise equality in society.[16]

The month of August came around, and Miss Allenville was to lay the foundation-stone of a tower or beacon which her father was about to erect on the highest hill of his estate, to the memory of his brother, the General. It was arranged that the school children should sing at the ceremony. Accordingly, at the hour fixed, Egbert was on the spot; a crowd of villagers had also arrived, and carriages were visible in the distance, wending their way towards the scene. When they had drawn up alongside and the visitors alighted, the master-mason appeared nervous.

'Mr. Mayne,' he said to Egbert, 'you had better do what's to be done for the lady. I shall speak too loud, or too soft, or handle things wrong. Do you attend upon her, and I'll lower the stone.'

Several ladies and gentlemen now gathered round, and presently Miss Allenville stood in position for her office, supported on one side by her father, a hard featured man of five-and-forty, and some friends who were visiting at the house; and on the other by the school children, who began singing a song in keeping

[16] Quoted from Thackeray's *Book of Snobs*, chapter 45 (originally " The Snobs of England " in *Punch*, 1847).

with the occasion. When this was done, Geraldine laid down the sealed bottle with its enclosed memorandum, which had been prepared for the purpose, and taking a trowel from her father's hand, dabbled confusedly in the mortar, accidentally smearing it over the handle of the trowel.

' Lower the stone,' said Egbert, who stood close by, to the mason at the winch; and the stone began to descend.

The dainty-handed young woman was looking as if she would give anything to be relieved of the dirty trowel; but Egbert, the only one who observed this, was guiding the stone with both hands into its place, and could not receive the tool of her. Every moment increased her perplexity.

' Take it, take it, will you? ' she impatiently whispered to him,[17] blushing with the consciousness that people began to perceive her awkward handling.

' I must just finish this first,' he said.

She was resigned in an instant. The stone settled down upon its base, when Egbert at once took the

[17] This is a reminiscence of an episode witnessed by Hardy in 1865. He had gone with his chief, Arthur Blomfield, to New Windsor to attend the laying of a memorial stone by the Crown Princess of Germany. Blomfield handed her the trowel, whereupon she soiled her glove with the mortar and in distress handed the trowel impatiently back to him, whispering, " Take it! take it! " Two years later Hardy transferred the words to Miss Allamont. (Cf. 23, p. 7.)

trowel, and her father came up and wiped her glove. Egbert then handed her the mallet.

'What must I do with this thing?' she whispered entreatingly, holding the mallet as if it might bite her.

'Tap with it, madam,' said he.

She did as was directed, and murmured the form of words which she had been told to repeat.

'Thank you,' she said softly when all was done, restored to herself by the consciousness that she had performed the last part gracefully. Without lifting her eyes she added, 'It was thoughtful of you to remember that I shouldn't know, and to stand by to tell me.'

Her friends now moved away, but before she had joined them Egbert said, chiefly for the pleasure of speaking to her: 'The tower, when it is built, will be seen many miles off.'

'Yes,' she replied in a discreet tone, for many eyes were upon her. 'The view is very extensive.' She glanced round upon the whole landscape stretched out before her, in the extreme distance of which was visible the town of Westcombe.[18]

'How long does it take to go to Westcombe across this way?' she asked of him while they were bringing up the carriage.

'About two hours,' he said.

[18] "Westcombe" was probably suggested by the name "Wool-comb,"—a property once owned by the senior branch of the Hardy family. (See *Early Life of Thomas Hardy*, p. 281.)

'Two hours — so long as that, does it? How far is it away?'

'Eight miles.'

'Two hours to drive eight miles — who ever heard of such a thing!'

'I thought you meant walking.'

'Ah, yes; but one hardly means walking without expressly stating it.'

'Well, it seems just the other way to me — that walking is meant unless you say driving.'

That was the whole of their conversation. The remarks had been simple and trivial, but they brought a similar thought into the minds of both of them. On her part it spread a sudden gloom over her face, and it made him feel dead at heart. It was that horrid thought of their differing habits and of those contrasting positions which could not be reconciled.

Indeed, this perception of their disparity weighed more and more heavily upon him as the days went on. There was no doubt about their being lovers, though scarcely recognised by themselves as such; and, in spite of Geraldine's warm and unreflecting impulses, a sense of how little Egbert was accustomed to what is called society, and the polite forms which constant usage had almost made nature with her, would rise on occasion, and rob her of many an otherwise pleasant minute. When any little occurrence had brought this into more prominence than usual, Egbert would go away, wander

about the lanes, and be kept awake a great part of the night by the distress of mind such a recognition brought upon him. How their intimacy would end, in what uneasiness, yearning, and misery, he could not guess. As for picturing a future of happiness with her by his side there was not ground enough upon which to rest the momentary imagination of it. Thus they mutually oppressed each other even while they loved.

In addition to this anxiety there was another; what would be thought of their romance by her father, if he were to find it out? It was impossible to tell him, for nothing could come of that but Egbert's dismissal and Geraldine's seclusion; and how could these be borne?

He looked round anxiously for some means of deliverance. There were two things to be thought of, the saving of her dignity, and the saving of his and her happiness. That to accomplish the first he ought voluntarily to leave the village before their attachment got known, and never seek her again, was what he sometimes felt; but the idea brought such misery along with it that it died out under contemplation.

He determined at all events to put the case clearly before her, to heroically set forth at their next meeting the true bearings of their position, which she plainly did not realise to the full as yet. It had never entered her mind that the link between them might be observed by the curious, and instantly talked of. Yes, it was his duty to warn her, even though by so doing he would

be heaping coals of fire on his own head. For by acting upon his hint she would be lost to him, and the charm that lay in her false notions of the world be for ever destroyed.

That they would ultimately be found out, and Geraldine be lowered in local estimation, was, indeed, almost inevitable. There was one grain of satisfaction only among this mass of distresses. Whatever should become public, only the fashionable side of her character could be depreciated; the natural woman, the specimen of English girlhood that he loved, no one could impugn or harm.

Meetings had latterly taken place between them without any pretence of accident, and these were facilitated in an amazing manner by the duty imposed upon her of visiting the school as the representative of her father. At her very next appearance he told her all he thought. It was when the children had left the room for the quarter of an hour's airing that he gave them in the middle of the morning.

She was quite hurt at being treated with justice, and a crowd of tears came into her sorrowful eyes. She had never thought of half that he feared, and almost questioned his kindness in enlightening her.

'Perhaps you are right,' she murmured, with the merest motion of lip. 'Yes, it is sadly true. Should our conduct become known, nobody will judge us fairly. "She was a wild, weak girl," they will say.'

'To care for such a man — a village youth. They will even suppress the fact that his father was a painter of no mean power, and a gentleman by education, little as it would redeem us; and justify their doing so by reflecting that in adding to the contrast they improve the tale.

> And calumny meanwhile shall feed on us
> As worms devour the dead: what we have done
> None shall dare vouch, though it be truly known.

And they will continue, " He was an artful fellow to win a girl's affections in that way — one of the mere scum of the earth," they'll say.'

'Don't, don't make it so bad!' she implored, weeping outright. 'They cannot go so far. Human nature is not so wicked and blind. And they *dare* not speak so disrespectfully of me, or of any one I choose to favour.' A slight haughtiness was apparent in these words. 'But, oh, don't let us talk of it — it makes the time miserable.'

However, she had been warned. But the difficulty which presented itself to her mind was, after all, but a small portion of the whole. It was how should they meet together without causing a convulsion in neighbouring society. His was more radical and complex. The only natural drift of love was towards marriage. But how could he picture, at any length of years ahead, her in a cottage as his wife, or himself in a mansion as

her husband? He in the one case, she in the other, were alike painfully incredible.

But time had flown, and he conducted her to the door. 'Good-bye, Egbert,' she said tenderly.

'Good-bye, dear, dear madam,' he answered; and she was gone.

Geraldine had never hinted to him to call her by her Christian name, and finding that she did not particularly wish it he did not care to do so. 'Madam' was as good a name as any other for her, and by adhering to it and using it at the warmest moments it seemed to change its nature from that of a mere title to a soft pet sound. He often wondered in after days at the strange condition of a girl's heart which could allow so much in reality, and at the same time permit the existence of a little barrier such as that; how the keen intelligent mind of woman could be ever so slightly hoodwinked by a sound. Yet, perhaps, it was womanlike, after all, and she may have caught at it as the only straw within reach of that dignity or pride of birth which was drowning in her impetuous affection.

## CHAPTER 8

The world and its ways have a certain worth,
And to press a point while these oppose
Were a simple policy: best wait,
And we lose no friends, and gain no foes.[19]

The inborn necessity of ransacking the future for a germ of hope led Egbert Mayne to dwell for longer and longer periods on the at first rejected possibility of winning and having her. And apart from any thought of marriage, he knew that Geraldine was sometimes a trifle vexed that their experiences contained so little in common—that he had never dressed for dinner, or made use of a carriage in his life; even though in literature he was her master, thanks to his tastes.

For the first time he seriously contemplated a visionary scheme which had been several times cursorily glanced at; a scheme almost as visionary as any ever entertained by a man not yet blinded to the limits of the possible. Lighted on by impulse, it was not taken up without long calculation, and it was one in which every link was reasoned out as carefully and as clearly as his powers would permit. But the idea that he

[19] Quoted from Browning's *The Statue and the Bust*, 138-141. Hardy thought this one of Browning's finest poems, and quoted from it four times in subsequent novels. When in Florence, Italy, Hardy visited the scene of this poem. See note 14 (p. 52).

would be able to carry it through was an assumption which, had he bestowed upon it one-hundredth part of the thought spent on the details of its working, he would have thrown aside as unfeasible.

To give up the school, to go to London or elsewhere, and there to try to rise to her level by years of sheer exertion, was the substance of this scheme. However his lady's heart might be grieved by his apparent desertion, he would go. A knowledge of life and of men must be acquired, and that could never be done by thinking at home.

Egbert's abstract love for the gigantic task was but small; but there was absolutely no other honest road to her sphere. That the habits of men should be so subversive of the law of nature as to indicate that he was not worthy to marry a woman whose own instincts said that he was worthy, was a great anomaly, he thought, with some rebelliousness; but this did not upset the fact or remove the difficulty.

He told his fair mistress at their next accidental meeting (much sophistry lay in their definition of ' accidental ' at this season) that he had determined to leave Tollamore. Mentally she exulted at his spirit, but her heart despaired. He solemnly assured her that it would be much better for them both in the end; and she became submissive, and entirely agreed with him. Then she seemed to acquire a sort of superior insight by

virtue of her superior rank, and murmured, 'You will expand your mind, and get to despise me for all this, and for my want of pride in being so easily won; and it will end unhappily.'

Her imagination so affected her that she could not hinder the tears from falling. Nothing was more effective in checking his despair than the sight of her despairing, and he immediately put on a more hopeful tone.

'No,' he said, taking her by the hand, 'I shall rise, and become so learned and so famous that—.' He did not like to say plainly that he really hoped to win her as his wife, but it is very probable that she guessed his meaning nearly enough.

'You have some secret resources!' she exclaimed. 'Some help is promised you in this ambitious plan.'

It was most painful to him to have to tell her the truth after this sanguine expectation, and how uncertain and unaided his plans were. However, he cheered her with the words, 'Wait and see.' But he himself had many misgivings when her sweet face was turned away.

Upon this plan he acted at once. Nothing of moment occurred during the autumn, and the time for his departure gradually came near. The sale of his grandfather's effects having taken place, and notice having been giving at the school, there was very little else for

him to do in way of preparation, for there was no family to be consulted, no household to be removed. On the last day of teaching, when the afternoon lessons were over, he bade farewell to the school children. The younger ones cried, not from any particular reflection on the loss they would sustain, but simply because their hearts were tender to any announcement couched in solemn terms. The elder children sincerely regretted Egbert, as an acquaintance who had not filled the post of schoolmaster so long as to be quite spoilt as a human being.

On the morning of departure he rose at half-past three, for Tollamore was a remote nook of a remote district, and it was necessary to start early, his plan being to go by packet from Melport.[20] The candle-flame had a sad and yellow look when it was brought into his bedroom by Nathan Brown, one of his grand-father's old labourers, at whose house he had taken a temporary lodging, and who had agreed to awake him and assist his departure. Few things will take away a man's confidence in an impulsive scheme more than being called up by candlelight upon a chilly morning to commence working it out. But when Egbert heard Nathan's great feet stamping spiritedly about the floor

[20] Hardy's name for Weymouth, a port about 14 or 15 miles from Stinsford. In later novels Hardy called this port Budmouth. See map, p. 85.

downstairs, in earnest preparation of breakfast, he overcame his weakness and bustled out of bed.

They breakfasted together, Nathan drinking the hot tea with rattling sips, and Egbert thinking as he looked at him that Nathan had never appeared so desirable a man to have about him as now when he was about to give him up.

'Well, good mornen, Mistur Mayne,' Nathan said, as he opened the door to let Egbert out. 'And mind this, sir; if they use ye bad up there, th'lt always find a hole to put thy head into at Nathan Brown's, I'll warrant as much.'

Egbert stepped from the door, and struck across to the manor-house. The morning was dark, and the raw wind made him shiver till walking warmed him. 'Good heavens, here's an undertaking!' he sometimes thought. Old trees seemed to look at him through the gloom, as they rocked uneasily to and fro; [21] and now and then a dreary drop of rain beat upon his face as he went on.

[21] The best evidence of Hardy's unique knowledge of trees was transferred from the "lost novel" and now appears in the first paragraph of *Under the Greenwood Tree*. See also his poem "In a Wood" (*Collected Poems*, p. 56). In a speech at the Society of Authors dinner, reported in the London *Morning Post* in January, 1929, Hardy's friend, Sir James M. Barrie, remarked of Hardy: "Everyone knows that he had an intimacy with trees surpassing even that of Giles Winterborne [in *The Woodlanders*]. . . . The trees had a similar knowledge of him. . . . When he passed through their wood, they could tell him from all other men!"

The dead leaves in the ditches, which could be heard but not seen, shifted their position with a troubled rustle, and flew at intervals with a little rap against his walking-stick and hat. He was glad to reach the north stile, and get into the park, where, with an anxious pulse, he passed beneath the creaking limes.

' Will she wake soon enough; will she be forgetful, and sleep over the time? ' He had asked himself this many times since he rose that morning, and still beset by the inquiry, he drew near to the mansion.[22]

Her bedroom was in the north wing, facing towards the church, and on turning the brow of the hill a faint light in the window reassured him. Taking a few little stones from the path he threw them upon the sill, as they had agreed, and she instantly opened the window, and said softly, ' The butler sleeps on the ground floor on this side, go to the bow-window in the shrubbery.'

He went round among the bushes to the place men-

[22] '; The mansion " would be described in some detail, if Hardy were here following his usual practice, or if we were not dealing with a fragmentary novel. Possibly the following description of " the mansion " originally appeared at this point in the text: —

" The house was regularly and substantially built of clear grey free-stone throughout, in that plainer fashion of classicism which prevailed at the latter end of the eighteenth century, when the copyists called designers had grown weary of fantastic variations in the Roman orders. The main block approximated to a square on the ground plan, having a projection in the center of each side, surmounted by a pediment. . . ." These words are taken from the description of " the mansion called Knapwater House " in *Desperate Remedies*, Chapter V, ii. (See p. 14 above.)

tioned, which was entirely sheltered from the wind. She soon appeared, bearing in her hand a wax taper, so small that it scarcely gave more light than a glow-worm. She wore the same dress that she had worn when they first met on the previous Christmas, and her hair was loose, at that time. Indeed, she looked throughout much as she had looked then, except that her bright eyes were red, as Egbert could see well enough.

'I have something for you,' she said softly as she opened the window. 'How much time is there?'

'Half-an-hour only, dearest.'

She began a sigh, but checked it, at the same time holding out a packet to him.

'Here are fifty pounds,' she whispered. 'It will be useful to you now, and more shall follow.'

Egbert felt how impossible it was to accept this. 'No, my dear one,' he said, 'I cannot.'

'I don't require it, Egbert. I wish you to have it; I have plenty. Come, do take it.' But seeing that he continued firm on this point she reluctantly gave in, saying that she would keep it for him.

'I fear so much that papa suspects me,' she said. 'And if so, it was my own fault, and all owing to a conversation I began with him without thinking before-hand that it would be dangerous.'

'What did you say?'

'I said,' she whispered, " Suppose a man should love

81

me very much, would you mind my being acquainted with him if he were a very worthy man?" "That depends upon his rank and circumstances," he said. "Suppose," I said, "that in addition to his goodness he had much learning, and he had made his name famous in the world, but was not altogether rich?" I think I showed too much earnestness, and I wished that I could have recalled my words. "When the time comes, I will tell you," he said, "and don't speak or think of these matters again."'

In consequence of this new imprudence of hers Egbert doubted if it would be right to correspond with her. He said nothing about it then, but it added a new shade to the parting.

'I think your decision a good and noble one,' she murmured, smiling hopefully. 'And you will come back some day a wondrous man of the world, talking of vast Schemes, radical Errors, and saying such words as the "Backbone of Society," the "Tendency of Modern Thought," and other things like that. When papa says to you, "My Lord the Chancellor," you will answer him with "A tall man, with a deep-toned voice—I know him well." When he says, "Such and such were Lord Hatton's words, I think," you will answer, "No, they were Lord Tyrrell's; I was present on the occasion"; and so on in that way. You must get to talk authoritatively about vintages and their

dates, and to know all about epicureanism, idleness, and fashion; and so you will beat him with his own weapons, for he knows nothing of these things. He will criticise you; then he will be nettled; then he will admire you.'

Egbert kissed her hand devotedly, and held it long.

'If you cannot in the least succeed,' she added, 'I shall never think the less of you. The truly great stand on no middling ledge; they are either famous or unknown.'

Egbert moved slowly away amongst the laurestines. Holding the light above her bright head she smiled upon him, as if it were unknown to her that she wept at the same time.

He left the park precincts, and followed the turnpike road to Melport. In spite of the misery of parting he felt relieved of a certain oppressiveness, now that his presence at Tollamore could no longer bring disgrace upon her. The threatening rain passed off by the time that he reached the ridge [23] dividing the inland districts from the coast. It began to get light, but his journey was still very lonely. Ultimately the yellow shore-line of pebbles grew visible, and the distant

[23] This ridge is called "the Ridgeway" in *Under the Greenwood Tree* (III, ii). See p. 14 above. In this novel the ridge is described as lying "between Budmouth and Mellstock,"—the Melport and Tollamore of this tale. The actual names are Weymouth and Stinsford, and the Ridgeway is the steep hill between the two, just north of Upwey. See map, p. 85.

horizon of water, spreading like a gray upland against the sky, till he could soon hear the measured flounce of the waves.

He entered the town at sunrise, just as the lamps were extinguished, and went to a tavern to breakfast. At half-past eight o'clock the boat steamed out of the harbour and reached London after a passage of five-and-forty hours.[24]

[24] Somewhat less than 300 miles.

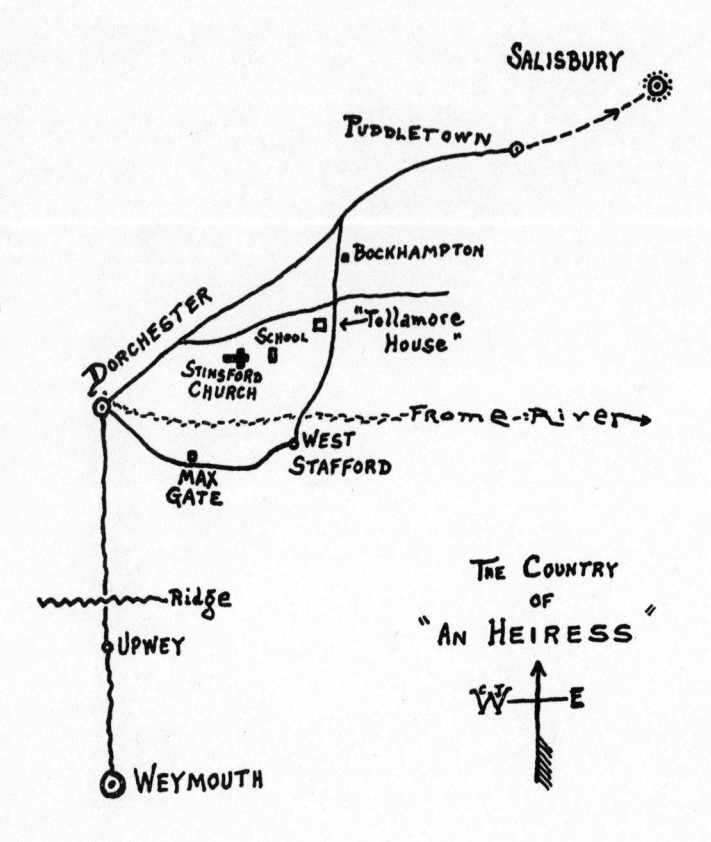

SALISBURY

PUDDLETOWN

BOCKHAMPTON

Dorchester

School

"Tollamore House"

Stinsford Church

Frome River

WEST STAFFORD

MAX GATE

THE COUNTRY OF "AN HEIRESS"

Ridge

UPWEY

WEYMOUTH

W E

# PART II

## CHAPTER 1

He, like a captain who beleaguers round
Some strong-built castle on a rising ground,
Views all the approaches with observing eyes;
This and that other part in vain he tries,
And more on industry than force relies.

Since Egbert Mayne's situation is not altogether a
new and unprecedented one, there will be no necessity
for detailing in all its minuteness his attempt to scale
the steeps of Fame. For notwithstanding the fact that
few, comparatively, have reached the top, the lower
tracts of that troublesome incline have been trodden by
as numerous a company as any allegorical spot in the
world.

The reader must then imagine five years to have
elapsed, during which rather formidable slice of human
life Egbert had been constantly striving. It had been
drive, drive from month to month; no rest, nothing
but effort. He had progressed from newspaper work
to criticism, from criticism to independent composition
of a mild order, from the latter to the publication of
a book which nobody ever heard of, and from this to
the production of a work of really sterling merit, which
appeared anonymously. Though he did not set society
in a blaze, or even in a smoke, thereby, he certainly

caused a good many people to talk about him, and to be curious as to his name.

The luminousness of nature which had been sufficient to attract the attention and heart of Geraldine Allenville had, indeed, meant much. That there had been power enough in the presence, speech, mind, and tone of the poor painter's son to fascinate a girl of Geraldine's station was of itself a ground for the presumption that he might do a work in the world if he chose. The attachment to her was just the stimulus which such a constitution as his required, and it had at first acted admirably upon him. Afterwards the case was scarcely so happy.

He had investigated manners and customs no less than literature; and for awhile the experience was exciting enough. But several habits which he had at one time condemned in the ambitious classes now became his own. His original fondness for art, literature, and science was getting quenched by his slowly increasing habit of looking upon each and all of these as machinery wherewith to effect a purpose.

A new feeling began to animate all his studies. He had not the old interest in them for their own sakes, but a breathless interest in them as factors in the game of sink or swim. He entered picture galleries, not, as formerly, because it was humour to dream pleasantly over the images therein expressed, but to be able to

talk on demand about painters and their peculiarities.[25] He examined Correggio to criticise his flesh shades; Angelico, to speak technically of the pink faces of his saints; Murillo, to say fastidiously that there was a certain silliness in the look of his old men; Rubens for his sensuous women; Turner for his Turneresqueness. Romney was greater than Reynolds because Lady Hamilton had been his model, and thereby hung a tale.[26] Bonozzi Gozzoli was better worth study than Raffaelle, since the former's name was a learned sound to utter, and all knowledge got up about him would tell.

Whether an intense love for a woman, and that woman Geraldine, was a justifiable reason for this desire to shine it is not easy to say.

However, as has been stated, Egbert worked like a slave in these causes, and at the end of five full years was repaid with certain public applause, though, unfortunately, not with much public money. But this he hoped might soon come.

Regarding his love for Geraldine, the most noteworthy fact to be recorded of the period was that all correspondence with her had ceased. In spite of their fear of her father, letters had passed frequently between

[25] For further illustrations of Hardy's extreme fondness for writing "about painters and their peculiarities," see E. Brennecke, *Life of Thomas Hardy*, New York, 1925, p. 110.

[26] Quoted from Shakespeare. It was a favorite remark of Hardy's favorite author. Cf. *Taming of the Shrew* (IV, i, 60); *Merry Wives* (I, iv, 155); *As You Like It* (II, vii, 28); and *Othello* (III, i, 8). See note 33, page 126.

them on his first leaving home, and had been continued with ardour for some considerable time. The reason of its close will be perceived in the following note, which he received from her two years before the date of the present chapter: —

'Tollamore House.

'My dear Egbert,

'How shall I tell you what has happened! and yet how can I keep silence when sooner or later you will know all?

'My father has discovered what we feel for each other. He took me into his room and made me promise never to write to you, or seek you, or receive a letter from you. I promised in haste, for I was frightened and excited, and now he trusts me—I wish he did not—for he knows I would not be mean enough to lie. So don't write, poor Egbert, or expect to hear from miserable me. We must try to hope; yet it is a long dreary thing to do. But I *will* hope, and not be beaten. How could I help promising, Egbert, when he compelled me? He is my father. I cannot think what we shall do under it all. It is cruel of life to be like this towards us when we have done no wrong.

\*     \*     \*     \*     \*

'We are going abroad for a long time. I think it is because of you and me, but I don't know. He does not tell me where we shall go. Just as if a place like Europe could make me forget you. He doesn't know what's in me, and how I can think about you and cry at nights—he cannot. If he did, he must see how silly the plan is.

'Remember that you go to church on Sunday mornings, for then I think that perhaps we are reading in the same place at the same moment; and we are sometimes, no doubt. Last

90

Sunday, when we came to this in the Psalms, "And he shall be like a tree planted by the waterside that will bring forth his fruit in due season: his leaf also shall not wither; and look, whatsoever he doeth, it shall prosper," I thought, "That's Egbert in London." I know you were reading that same verse in your church—I felt that you said it with us. Then I looked up to your old nook under the tower arch. It was a misery to see the wood and the stone just as good as ever, and you not there. It is not only that you are gone at these times, but a heavy creature—blankness—seems to stand in your place.

' But how can I tell you of these thoughts now that I am to write no more? Yet we will hope, and hope. Remember this, that should anything serious happen, I will break the bond and write. Obligation would end then. Good-bye for a time. I cannot put into words what I would finish with. Good-bye, good-bye.

'G. A.

' P. S. Might we not write just one line at very wide intervals? It is too much never to write at all.'

On receiving this letter Egbert felt that he could not honourably keep up a regular correspondence with her. But a determination to break it off would have been more than he could have adhered to if he had not been strengthened by the hope that he might soon be able to give a plausible reason for renewing it. He sent her a line, bidding her to expect the best results from the prohibition, which, he was sure, would not be for long. Meanwhile, should she think it not wrong to send a line at very wide intervals, he would promptly reply.

But she was apparently too conscientious to do so, for nothing had reached him since. Yet she was as continually in his thought and heart as before. He felt more misgivings than he had chosen to tell her of on the ultimate effect of the prohibition, but could do nothing to remove it. And then he had learnt that Miss Allenville and her father had gone to Paris, as the commencement of a sojourn abroad.

These circumstances had burdened him with long hours of depression, till he had resolved to throw his whole strength into a production which should either give him a fair start towards fame, or make him clearly understand that there was no hope in that direction for such as he. He had begun the attempt, and ended it, and the consequences were fortunate to an unexpected degree.

## CHAPTER 2

Towards the loadstar of my one desire
I flitted like a dizzy moth, whose flight
Is as a dead leaf's in the owlet light. [26a]

Mayne's book having been launched into the world and well received, he found time to emerge from the seclusion he had maintained for several months, and to look into life again.

One warm, fashionable day, between five and six o'clock, he was walking along Piccadilly, absent-minded and unobservant, when an equipage approached whose appearance thrilled him through. It was the Allenville landau, newly-painted up. Egbert felt almost as if he had been going into battle; and whether he should stand forth visibly before her or keep in the background seemed a question of life or death.

He waited in unobserved retirement, which it was not difficult to do, his aspect having much altered since the old times. Coachman, footman, and carriage advanced, in graceful unity of glide, like a swan. Then he beheld her, Geraldine, after two years of silence, five years of waiting, and nearly three years of separation; for although he had seen her two or three times in town after he had taken up his residence there, they

[26a] Quoted from P. B. Shelley's *Epipsychidion*, lines 219-221. Hardy again quoted these same lines in *The Woodlanders* (1886), chapter 28.

had not once met since the year preceding her departure for the Continent.

She came opposite, now passively looking round, then actively glancing at something which interested her. Egbert trembled a little, or perhaps a great deal, at sight of her. But she passed on, and the back of the carriage hid her from his view.

So much of the boy was left in him still that he could scarcely withhold himself from rushing after her, and jumping into the carriage. She had appeared to be well and blooming, and an instinctive vexation that their long separation had produced no perceptible effect upon her, speedily gave way before a more generous sense of gratification at her well-being. Still, had it been possible, he would have been glad to see some sign upon her face that she yet remembered him.

This sudden discovery that they were in town after their years of travel stirred his lassitude into excitement. He went back to his chambers to meditate upon his next step. A trembling on Geraldine's account was disturbing him. She had probably been in London ever since the beginning of the season, but she had not given him a sign to signify that she was so near; and but for this accidental glimpse of her he might have gone on for months without knowing that she had returned from abroad.

Whether she was leading a dull or an exciting life Egbert had no means of knowing. That night after

night the arms of interesting young men rested upon her waist and whirled her round the ball-room he could not bear to think. That she frequented gatherings and assemblies of all sorts he calmly owned as very probable, for she was her father's only daughter, and likely to be made much of. That she had not written a line to him since their return was still the grievous point.

'If I had only risen one or two steps further,' he thought, 'how boldly would I seek her out. But only to have published one successful book in all these years — such grounds are slight indeed.'

For several succeeding days he did nothing but look about the Park, and the streets, and the neighbourhood of Chevron Square, where their town-house stood, in the hope of seeing her again; but in vain. There were moments when his distress that she might possibly be indifferent about him and his affairs was unbearable. He fully resolved that he would on some early occasion communicate with her, and know the worst. Years of work remained to be done before he could think of appearing before her father; but he had reached a sort of half-way stage at which some assurance from herself that his track was a hopeful one was positively needed to keep him firm.

Egbert still kept on the look-out for her at every public place; but nearly a month passed, and she did not appear again. One Sunday evening, when he had been wandering near Chevron Square, and looking at

her windows from a distance, he returned past her house after dusk. The rooms were lighted, but the windows were still open, and as he strolled along he heard notes from a piano within. They were the accompaniment to an air from the *Messiah*, though no singer's voice was audible. Egbert readily imagined who the player might be, for the *Messiah* was an oratorio which Geraldine often used to wax eloquent upon in days gone by. He had not walked far when he remembered that there was to be an exceptionally fine performance of that stirring composition during the following week, and it instantly occurred to him that Geraldine's mind was running on the same event, and that she intended to be one of the audience.

He resolved upon doing something at a venture. The next morning he went to the ticket-office, and boldly asked for a place as near as possible to those taken in the name of Allenville.

' There is no vacant one in any of those rows,' the office-keeper said, ' but you can have one very near their number on the other side of the division.'

Egbert was astonished that for once in his life he had made a lucky hit. He booked his place, and returned home.

The evening arrived, and he went early. On taking his seat he found himself at the left-hand end of a

series of benches, and close to a red cord, which divided the group of seats he had entered from stalls of a somewhat superior kind. He was passing the time in looking at the extent of orchestra space, and other things, when he saw two ladies and a gentleman enter and sit down in the stalls diagonally before his own, and on the other side of the division. It delighted and agitated him to find that one of the three was Geraldine; her two companions he did not know.

' Policy, don't desert me now,' he thought; and immediately sat in such a way that unless she turned round to a very unlikely position she would not see him.

There was a certain half-pleasant misery in sitting behind her thus as a possibly despised lover. Tonight, at any rate, there would be sights and sounds common to both of them, though they should not communicate to the extent of a word. Even now he could hear the rustle of her garments as she settled down in her seat, and the faint murmur of words that passed between her and her friends.

Never, in the many times that he had listened to that rush of harmonies, had they affected him as they did then; and it was no wonder, considering what an influence upon his own life had been and still was exercised by Geraldine, and that she now sat there before him. The varying strains shook and bent him to them-

selves as a rippling brook shakes and bends a shadow. The music did not show its power by attracting his attention to its subject; it rather dropped its own libretto and took up in place of that the poem of his life and love.

There was Geraldine still. They were singing the chorus ' Lift up your heads,' and he found a new impulse of thought in him. It was towards determination. Should every member of her family be against him he would win her in spite of them. He could now see that Geraldine was moved equally with himself by the tones which entered her ears.

' Why do the nations so furiously rage together' filled him with a gnawing thrill, and so changed him to its spirit that he believed he was capable of suffering in silence for his whole lifetime, and of never appearing before her unless she gave a sign.

The audience stood up, and the ' Hallelujah Chorus ' began. The deafening harmonies flying from this group and from that seemed to absorb all the love and poetry that his life had produced, to pour it upon that one moment, and upon her who stood so close at hand. ' I will force Geraldine to be mine,' he thought. ' I will make that heart ache of love for me.' The chorus continued, and her form trembled under its influence. Egbert was for seeking her the next morning and knowing what his chances were, without waiting for further results. The chorus and the personality of

Geraldine still filled the atmosphere. 'I will seek her tonight — as soon as we get out of this place,' he said. The storm of sound now reached its climax, and Geraldine's power was proportionately increased. He would give anything for a glance this minute — to look into her eyes, she into his. 'If I can but touch her hand, and get one word from her, I will,' he murmured.

He shifted his position somewhat and saw her face. Tears were in her eyes, and her lips were slightly parted. Stretching a little nearer he whispered, 'My love!'

Geraldine turned her wet eyes upon him, almost as if she had not been surprised, but had been forewarned by her previous emotion. With the peculiar quickness of grasp that she always showed under sudden circumstances, she had realised the position at a glance.

'Oh, Egbert!' she said; and her countenance flagged as if she would have fainted.

'Give me your hand,' he whispered.

She placed her hand in his, under the cord, which it was easy to do without observation; and he held it tight.

'Mine, as before?' he asked.

'Yours now as then,' said she.

They were like frail and sorry wrecks upon that sea of symphony, and remained in silent abandonment to the time, till the strains approached their close.

'Can you meet me tonight?' said Egbert.

She was half frightened at the request, and said,
'Where?'

'At your own front door, at twelve o'clock.' He then
was at once obliged to gently withdraw himself, for the
chorus was ended, and the people were sitting down.

The remainder was soon over, and it was time to
leave. Egbert watched her and her party out of the
house, and, turning to the other doorway, went out
likewise.

## CHAPTER 3

Bright reason will mock thee,
Like the sun from a wintry sky.

When he reached his chambers he sat down and literally did nothing but watch the hand of the mantel-clock minute by minute, till it marked half-past eleven, scarcely removing his eyes. Then going again into the street he called a cab, and was driven down Park Lane and on to the corner of Chevron Square. Here he alighted, and went round to the number occupied by the Allenvilles.

A lamp stood nearly opposite the doorway, and by receding into the gloom to the railing of the square he could see whatever went on in the porch of the house. The lamps over the doorways were nearly all extinguished, and everything about this part was silent and deserted, except at a house on the opposite side of the square, where a ball was going on. But nothing of that concerned Egbert: his eyes had sought out and remained fixed upon Mr. Allenville's front door, in momentary expectation of seeing it gently open.

The dark wood of the door showed a keen and distinct edge upon the pale stone of the porch floor. It must have been about two minutes before the hour he had named when he fancied he saw a slight movement

at that point, as of something slipped out from under the door.

' It is but fancy,' he said to himself.

He turned his eyes away, and turned them back again. Some object certainly seemed to have been thrust under the door. At this moment the four quarters of midnight began to strike, and then the hour. Egbert could remain still no longer, and he went into the porch. A note had been slipped under the door from inside.

He took it to the lamp, turned it over, and saw it was directed only with initials,—' To E. M.' Egbert tore it open and glanced upon the page. With a shiver of disappointment he read these words in her hand-writing:—

' It was when under the influence of much emotion, kindled in me by the power of the music, that I half assented to a meeting with you tonight; and I believe that you also were excited when you asked for one. After some quiet reflection I have decided that it will be much better for us both if we do not see each other.

' You will, I know, judge me fairly in this. You have by this time learnt what life is; what particular positions, accidental though they may be, ask, nay, imperatively exact from us. If you say " not imperatively," you cannot speak from knowledge of the world.

' To be woven and tied in with the world by blood, acquaintance, tradition, and external habit, is to a woman to be utterly at the beck of that world's customs. In youth we do not see

this. You and I did not see it. We were but a girl and a boy at the time of our meetings at Tollamore. What was our knowledge? A list of other people's words. What was our wisdom? None at all.

'It is well for you to remember now that I am not the unsophisticated girl I was when you first knew me. For better or for worse I have become complicated, exclusive, and practised. A woman who can speak, or laugh, or dance, or sing before any number of men with perfect composure may be no sinner, but she is not what I was once. She is what I am now. She is not the girl you loved. That woman is not here.

'I wish to write kindly to you, as to one for whom, in spite of the unavoidable division between our paths, I must always entertain a heartfelt respect. Is it, after this, out of place in me to remind you how contrasting are all our associations, how inharmonious our times and seasons? Could anything ever overpower this incongruity?

'But I must write plainly, and, though it may grieve you now, it will produce ultimately the truest ease. This is my meaning. If I could accept your addresses without an entire loss of position I would do so; but, since this cannot be, we must forget each other.

'Believe me to be, with wishes and prayers for your happiness,

'Your sincere friend,
'G. A.'

Egbert could neither go home nor stay still; he walked off rapidly in any direction for the sole sake of vehement motion. His first impulse was to get into darkness. He went towards Kensington; thence

threaded across to the Uxbridge Road, thence to Kensal Green, where he turned into a lane and followed it to Kilburn, and the hill beyond, at which spot he halted and looked over the vast haze of light extending to the length and breadth of London. Turning back and wandering among some fields by a way he could never afterwards recollect, sometimes sitting down, sometimes leaning on a stile, he lingered on until the sun had risen. He then slowly walked again towards London, and, feeling by this time very weary, he entered the first refreshment-house that he came to, and attempted to eat something. Having sat for some time over this meal without doing much more than taste it, he arose and set out for the street in which he lived. Once in his own rooms he lay down upon the couch and fell asleep.

When he awoke it was four o'clock. Egbert then dressed and went out, partook of a light meal at his club at the dismal hour between luncheon and dinner, and cursorily glanced over the papers and reviews. Among the first things that he saw were eulogistic notices of his own book in three different reviews, each the most prominent and weighty of its class. Two of them, at least, would, he knew, find their way to the drawing room of the Allenvilles, for they were among the periodicals which the Squire regularly patronised.

Next, in a weekly review he read the subjoined note:—

' The authorship of the book ―― ――, about which con-
jecture has lately been so much exercised, is now ascribed to
Mr. Egbert Mayne, whose first attempt in that kind we noticed
in these pages some eighteen months ago.'

He took up a daily paper and presently lighted on
the following paragraph:—

' It is announced that a marriage is arranged between Lord
Bretton, of Tosthill Park, and Geraldine, only daughter of
Foy [27] Allenville, Esq., of Tollamore House, Wessex.' [28]

Egbert arose and went towards home. Arrived there
he met the postman at the door, and received from him
a small note. The young man mechanically glanced at
the direction.

' From her,' he mentally exclaimed: ' What does
it ――'

This was what the letter contained:—

' Twelve o'clock.

' I have just learnt that the anonymous author of the book
in which the world has been so interested during the past two

---

[27] " Foy " may be surmised to be an 1878 misprint for the 1868
" Fay," the latter a common-enough name which Hardy had certainly
first used. See p. 6, No. 9. The change from " Allamont " to " Allenville " is wholly in keeping with Hardy's practice of re-naming persons
and places when revising his novels. See Carl J. Weber, " The Manuscript Names of Hardy's Characters," *Review of English Studies* (10:
456-459), October, 1934.

[28] " Wessex ": this now well-known word was only four years old
(in the Hardian sense) at the time it appeared in this tale. Hardy had
first used it in *Far From the Madding Crowd* in 1874.

months, and which I have read, is none other than yourself. Accept my congratulations. It seems almost madness in me to address you now. But I could not do otherwise on receipt of this news, and after writing my last letter. Let your knowledge of my nature prevent your misconstruing my motives in writing thus on the spur of the moment. I need scarcely add, please keep it a secret forever. I am not morally afraid, but other lives, hopes, and objects than mine have to be considered.

'The announcement of the marriage is premature, to say the least. I would tell you more, but dare not.      'G. A.'

The conjunction of all this intelligence produced in Egbert's heart a stillness which was some time in getting aroused to excitement. His emotion was formless. He knew not what point to take hold of and survey his position from; and, though his faculties grew clearer with the passage of time, he failed in resolving on a course with any deliberateness. No sooner had he thought, ' I will never see her again for my pride's sake,' than he said, ' Why not see her? she is a woman; she may love me yet.'

He went down stairs and out of the house, and walked by way of the Park towards Chevron Square.

Probably nobody will rightly appreciate Mayne's wild behaviour at this juncture, unless, which is very unlikely, he has been in a somewhat similar position himself. It may always appear to cool critics, even if they are generous enough to make allowances for his

feelings, as visionary and weak in the extreme. Yet it was scarcely to be expected, after the mental and emotional strain that he had undergone during the preceding five years, that he should have acted much otherwise.

He rang the bell and asked to see Mr. Allenville. He, perhaps fortunately, was not at home. 'Miss Allenville, then,' said Mayne.

'She is just driving out,' said the footman dubiously.

Egbert then noticed for the first time that the carriage was at the door, and almost as soon as the words were spoken Geraldine came downstairs.

'The madness of hoping to call that finished creature, wife!' he thought.

Geraldine recognised him and looked perplexed.

'One word, Miss Allenville,' he murmured.

She assented, and he followed her into the adjoining room.

'I have come,' said Egbert. 'I know it is hasty of me; but I must hear my doom from your own lips. Five years ago you spurred me on to ambition. I have followed but too closely the plan I then marked out, for I have hoped all along for a reward. What am I to think? Have you indeed left off feeling what you once felt for me?'

'I cannot speak of it now,' she said hurriedly. 'I told you in my letter as much as I dared. Believe me

107

I cannot speak—in the way you wish. I will always be your friend.'

' And is this the end? Oh, my God! '

' And we shall hope to see you to dinner some day, now you are famous,' she continued, pale as ashes. ' But I — cannot be with you as we once were. I was such a child at that time, you know.'

' Geraldine, is this all I get after this lapse of time and heat of labour? '

' I am not my own mistress—I have my father to please,' she faintly murmured. 'I must please him. There is no help for this. Go from me—do go! '

Egbert turned and went, for he felt that he had no longer a place beside her.

## CHAPTER 4

Then I said in my heart, ' As it happeneth to the fool, so it happeneth even to me; and why was I then more wise?' [29]

Mayne was in rather an ailing state for several days after the above-mentioned event. Yet the lethean stagnation which usually comes with the realisation that all is over allowed him to take some deep sleeps, to which he latterly had been a stranger.

The hours went by, and he did the best he could to dismiss his regrets for Geraldine. He was assisted to the very little success that he attained in this by reflecting how different a woman she must have become from her old sweet self of five or six years ago.

' But how paltry is my success now she has vanished! ' he said. ' What is it worth? What object have I in following it up after this?' It rather startled him to see that the root of his desire for celebrity having been Geraldine, he now was a man who had no further motive in moving on. Town life had for some time been depressing to him. He began to doubt whether he could ever be happy in the course of existence that he had followed through these later years. The perpetual strain, the lack of that quiet to which he had been

[29] Quoted from the Bible: *Ecclesiastes*, II, 15. For information regarding a study of Hardy's great indebtedness to the King James Bible, see *Shakespeare Association Bulletin*, April, 1934, p. 92.

accustomed in early life, the absence of all personal interest in things around him, was telling upon his health of body and of mind.

Then revived the wish which had for some time been smouldering in his secret heart—to leave off, for the present, at least, his efforts for distinction; to retire for a few months to his old country nook, and there to meditate on his next course.

To set about this was curiously awkward to him. He had planned methods of retrogression in case of defeat through want of ability, want of means, or lack of opportunity; but to retreat because his appetite for advance had gone off was what he had never before thought of.

His reflections turned upon the old home of his mother's family. He knew exactly how Tollamore appeared at that time of the year. The trees with their half-ripe apples, the bees and butterflies lazy from the heat; the haymaking over, the harvest not begun, the people lively and always out of doors. He would visit the spot, and call upon some old and half-forgotten friends of his grandfather in an adjoining parish.

Two days later he left town. The fine weather, his escape from that intricate web of effort in which he had been bound these five years, the sensation that nobody in the world had any claims upon him, imparted some buoyancy to his mind; and it was in a serene if sad

spirit that he entered Tollamore Vale, and smelt his native air.

He did not at once proceed to the village, but stopped at Fairland,[30] the parish next adjoining. It was now evening, and he called upon some of the old cottagers whom he knew. Time had set a mark upon them all since he had last been there. Middle-aged men were a little more round-shouldered, their wives had taken to spectacles, young people had grown up out of recognition, and old men had passed into second childhood.

Egbert found here, as he had expected, precisely such a lodging as a hermit would desire. It was an ivy-covered detached house which had been partly furnished for a tenant who had never come, and it was kept clean by an old woman living in a cottage near. She offered to wait upon Egbert whilst he remained there, coming in the morning and leaving in the afternoon, thus giving him the house to himself during the latter part of the day.

When it grew dusk he went out, wishing to ramble for a little time. The gibbous moon rose on his right, the stars showed themselves sleepily one by one, and the far distance turned to a mysterious ocean of grey. He instinctively directed his steps toward Tollamore, and when there towards the school. It looked very

[30] Possibly suggested by Bockhampton, Hardy's native parish, which adjoins Stinsford. See map, p. 85.

little changed since the year in which he had had the memorable meetings with her there, excepting that the creepers had grown higher.

He went on towards the Park. Here was the place whereon he had used to await her coming—he could be sure of the spot to a foot. There was the turn of the hill around which she had appeared. The sentimental effect of the scenes upon him was far greater than he had expected, so great that he wished he had never been so reckless as to come here. ' But this is folly,' he thought. ' The betrothed of Lord Bretton is a woman of the world in whose thoughts, hopes, and habits I have no further interest or share.'

In the lane he heard the church-bells ringing out their five notes, and meeting a shepherd Egbert asked him what was going on.

' Practising,' he said, in an uninterested voice. ' 'Tis against young Miss's wedding, that their hands may be thoroughly in by the day for't.'

He presently came to where his grandfather's old house had stood. It was pulled down, the ground it covered having become a shabby, irregular spot, half grown over with trailing plants. The garden had been grassed down, but the old apple-trees still remained, their trunks and stems being now sheeted on one side with moonlight. He entertained himself by guessing where the front door of the house had been, at which

Geraldine had entered on the memorable evening when she came to him full of grief and pity, and a tacit avowal of love was made on each side. Where they had sat together was now but a heap of broken rubbish half covered with grass. Near this melancholy spot was the cottage once inhabited by Nathan Brown. But Nathan was dead now, and his wife and family had gone elsewhere.

Finding the effect of memory to be otherwise than cheerful, Mayne hastened from the familiar spot, and went on to the parish of Fairland in which he had taken his lodging.

It soon became whispered in the neighbourhood that Miss Allenville's wedding was to take place on the 17th of October.[31] Egbert heard few particulars of the matter beyond the date, though it is possible that he might have known more if he had tried. He preferred to fortify himself by dipping deeply into the few books he had brought with him; but the most obvious plan of escaping his thoughts, that of a rapid change of scene by travel, he was unaccountably loth to adopt. He felt that he could not stay long in this district; yet an indescribable fascination held him on day after day, till the date of the marriage was close at hand.

[31] See note 11, p. 45.

## CHAPTER 5

How all the other passions fleet to air,
As doubtful thoughts, and rash-embraced despair
And shudd'ring fear, and green-eyed jealousy! [32]

On the eve of the wedding people told Mayne that
arches and festoons of late summer-flowers and ever-
greens had been put up across the path between the
church porch at Tollamore and the private gate to the
Squire's lawn, for the procession of bride and brides-
maids. Before it got dark several villagers went on
foot to the church to look at and admire these decora-
tions. Egbert had determined to see the ceremony over.
It would do him good, he thought, to be witness of the
sacrifice.

Hence he, too, went along the path to Tollamore to
inspect the preparations. It was dusk by the time that
he reached the churchyard, and he entered it boldly,
letting the gate fall together with a loud slam, as if
he were a man whom nothing troubled. He looked at
the half-completed bowers of green, and passed on
into the church, never having entered it since he first
left Tollamore.

He was standing by the chancel-arch, and observing
the quantity of flowers which had been placed around
the spot, when he heard the creaking of a gate on its

[32] Quoted from Shakespeare's *Merchant of Venice* (III, ii, 108). See
note 33, p. 126.

114

hinges. Two figures entered the church, and Egbert stepped behind a canopied tomb.

The persons were females, and they appeared to be servants from the neighbouring mansion. They brought more flowers and festoons, and were talking of the event of the morrow. Coming into the chancel they threw down their burdens with a remark that it was too dark to arrange more flowers that night.

'This is where she is to kneel,' said one, standing with her arms akimbo before the altar-railing. 'And I wish 'twas I instead, Lord send if I don't.'

The two girls went on gossiping until other footsteps caused them to turn.

'I won't say 'tisn't she. She has been here two or three times today. Let's go round this way.'

And the servants went towards the door by a circuitous path round the aisle, to avoid meeting with the new-comer.

Egbert, too, thought he would leave the place now that he had heard and seen thus much; but from carelessness or design he went straight down the nave. An instant afterwards he was standing face to face with Geraldine. The servants had vanished.

'Good evening,' she said serenely, not knowing him, and supposing him to be a parishioner.

Egbert returned the words hastily, and, in standing aside to let her pass, looked clearly into her eyes and

pale face, as if there never had been a time at which he would have done anything on earth for her sake.

She knew him, and started, uttering a weak exclamation. When he reached the door he turned his head, and saw that she was irresolutely holding up her hand, as if to beckon to him to come back.

' One word, since I have met you,' she said in unequal half-whispered tones. ' I have felt that I was one-sided in my haste on the day you called to see me in London. I misunderstood you.'

Egbert could at least out-do her in self-control, and, astonished that she should have spoken, he answered in a yet colder tone,

' I am sorry for that; very sorry, madam.'

' And you excuse it? '

' Of course I do, readily. And I hope you, too, will pardon my intrusion on that day, and understand the— circumstances.'

' Yes, yes. Especially as I am most to blame for those indiscreet proceedings in our early lives which led to it.'

' Certainly you were not most to blame.'

' How can you say that? ' she answered with a slight laugh, ' when you know nothing of what my motives and feelings were? '

' I know well enough to judge, for I was the elder. Let me just recall some points in your own history at that time.'

' No.'

'Will you not hear a word?'

'I cannot . . . Are you writing another book?'

'I am doing nothing. I am idling at Monk's Hut.'

'Indeed!' she said, slightly surprised. 'Well, you will always have my good wishes, whatever you may do. If any of my relatives can ever help you —'

'Thank you, madam, very much. I think, however, that I can help myself.'

She was silent, looking upon the floor; and Egbert spoke again, successfully hiding the feelings of his heart under a light and untrue tone. 'Miss Allenville, you know that I loved you devotedly for many years, and that that love was the starting point of all my ambition. My sense of it makes this meeting rather awkward. But men survive almost anything. I have proved it. Their love is strong while it lasts, but it soon withers at sight of a new face. I congratulate you on your coming marriage. Perhaps I may marry some day, too.'

'I hope you will find someone worth your love. I am sorry I ever — inconvenienced you as I did. But one hardly knows at that age —'

'Don't think of it for a moment — I really entreat you not to think of that.' What prompted the cruelty of his succeeding words he never could afterwards understand. 'It was a hard matter at first for me forget you, certainly; but perhaps I was helped in my wish by the strong prejudice I originally had against your class

and family. I have fixed my mind firmly upon the differences between us, and my youthful fancy is pretty fairly overcome. Those old silly days of devotion were pretty enough, but the devotion was entirely unpractical, as you have seen, of course.'

'Yes, I have seen it,' she faltered.

'It was scarcely of a sort which survives accident and division, and is strengthened by disaster.'

'Well, perhaps not, perhaps not. You can scarcely care much now whether it was or not; or, indeed, care anything about me or my happiness.'

'I do care.'

'How much? As you do for that of any other wretched human being?'

'Wretched? No!'

'I will tell you — I must tell you!' she said with rapid utterance. 'This is my secret, this. I don't love the man I am going to marry; but I have agreed to be his wife to satisfy my friends. Say you don't hate me for what I have told. I could not bear that you should know!'

'Hate you? Oh, Geraldine!'

A hair's-breadth further, and they would both have broken down.

'Not a word more. Now you know my unhappy state, and I shall die content.'

'But, darling — my Geraldine!'

'It is too late. Good-night — good-bye!' She spoke in a hurried voice, almost like a low cry, and rushed away.

Here was a revelation. Egbert moved along to the door, and up the path, in a condition in which his mind caused his very body to ache. He gazed vacantly through the railings of the lawn, which came close to the churchyard; but she was gone. He still moved mechanically on. A little further and he was overtaken by the parish clerk, who, addressing a few words to him, soon recognised his voice.

The clerk's talk, too, was about the wedding. 'Is the marriage likely to be a happy one?' asked Egbert, aroused by the subject.

'Well, between you and me, Mr. Mayne, 'tis a made up affair. Some says she can't bear the man.'

'Lord Bretton?'

'Yes. I could say more if I dared; but what's the good of it now!'

'I suppose none,' said Egbert wearily.

He was glad to be alone again, and went on towards Fairland slowly and heavily. Had Geraldine forgotten him, and loved elsewhere with a light heart, he could have borne it; but this sacrifice at a time when, left to herself, she might have listened to him, was an intolerable misery. Her inconsistent manner, her appearance of being swayed by two feelings, her half-reservations

were all explained. 'Against her wishes,' he said; 'at heart she may still be mine. Oh, Geraldine, my poor Geraldine, is it come to this!'

He bitterly regretted his first manner towards her, and turned round to consider whether he could not go back, endeavour to find her, and ask if he could be of any possible use. But all this was plainly absurd. He again proceeded homeward as before.

Reaching Fairland he sat awhile in his empty house without a light, and then went to bed. Owing to the distraction of his mind he lay for three or four hours meditating, and listening to the autumn wind, turning restlessly from side to side, the blood throbbing in his temples and singing in his ears, and the ticking of his watch waxing apparently loud enough to stun him. He conjured up the image of Geraldine in her various stages of preparation on the following day. He saw her coming in at the well-known door, walking down the aisle in a floating cloud of white, and receiving the eyes of the assembled crowd without a flush, or a sign of consciousness; uttering the words, 'I take thee to my wedded husband,' as quietly as if she were dreaming them. And the husband? Egbert shuddered. How could she have consented, even if her memories stood their ground only half so obstinately as his own? As for himself, he perceived more clearly than ever how intricately she had mingled with every motive in his past career. Some portion of the thought, 'marriage

with Geraldine,' had been marked on every day of his manhood.

Ultimately he fell into a fitful sleep, when he dreamed of fighting, wading, diving, boring, through innumerable multitudes, in the midst of which Geraldine's form appeared flitting about, in the usual confused manner of dreams, — sometimes coming towards him, sometimes receding, and getting thinner and thinner till she was a mere film tossed about upon a seething mass.

He jumped up in the bed, damp with a cold perspiration, and in an agony of disquiet. It was a minute or two before he could collect his senses. He went to the window and looked out. It was quite dark, and the wind moaned and whistled round the corners of the house in the heavy intonations which seem to express that ruthlessness has all the world to itself.

' Egbert, do, do come to me! ' reached his ears in a faint voice from the darkness.

There was no mistaking it: it was assuredly the tongue of Geraldine.

He half dressed himself, ran down stairs, and opened the front door, holding the candle above his head. Nobody was visible.

He set down the light, hastened round the back of the house, and saw a dusky figure turning the corner to get to the gate. He then ran diagonally across the plot, and intercepted the form in the path. ' Geraldine! ' he said, ' can it indeed be you? '

121

'Yes, it is, it is!' she cried wildly, and fell upon his shoulder.

The hot turmoil of excitement pervading her hindered her from fainting, and Egbert placed his arm round her, and led her into the house, without asking a question, or meeting with any resistance. He assisted her into a chair as soon as they reached the front room.

'I have run away from home, Egbert, and to you!' she sobbed. 'I am not insane: they and you may think so, but I am not. I came to find you. Such shocking things have happened since I met you just now. Can Lord Bretton come and claim me?'

'Nobody on earth can claim you, darling, against your will. Now tell it all to me.'

She spoke on between her tears. 'I have loved you ever since, Egbert; but such influences have been brought to bear upon me that at last I have hardly known what I was doing. At last, I thought that perhaps, after all, it would be better to become a lady of title, with a large park and houses of my own, than the wife of any man of genius who was poor. I loved you all the time, but I was half ashamed that I loved you. I went out continually, that gaiety might obscure the past. And then dark circles came round my eyes — I grew worn and tired. I am not nearly so nice to look at as at that time when we used to meet in the school, nor so healthy either. . . . I think I was handsome

then.' At this she smiled faintly, and raised her eyes
to his, with a sparkle of their old mischief in them.

'And now and ever,' he whispered.

'How innocent we were then! Fancy, Egbert, our
unreserve would have been almost wrong if we had
known the canons of behaviour we learnt afterwards.
Ah! who at that time would have thought I was to
yield to what I did? I wish now that I had met you
at the door in Chevron Square, as I promised. But I
feared to — I had promised Lord Bretton — and I that
evening received a lecturing from my father, who saw
you at the concert — he was in a seat further behind.
And then, when I heard of your great success, how I
wished I had held out a little longer! for I knew your
hard labour had been on my account. When we met
again last night it seemed awful, horrible—what I had
done. Yet how could I tell you plainly? When I got
indoors I felt I should die of misery, and I went to my
father, and said I could not be married tomorrow. Oh,
how angry he was and what a dreadful scene occurred!'
She covered her face with her hands.

'My poor Geraldine!' said Egbert, supporting her
with his arm.

'When I was in my room this came into my mind,
" Better is it that thou shouldst not vow, than that thou
shouldst vow and not pay." I could bear it no longer.
I was determined not to marry him, and to see you

again, whatever came of it. I dressed, and came down
stairs noiselessly, and slipped out. I knew where your
house was, and hastened here.'

'You will never marry him now?'

'Never. Yet what can I do? Oh! what can I do?
If I go back to my father—no, I cannot go back now—
it is too late. But if they should find me, and drag me
back, and compel me to perform my promise!'

'There is one simple way to prevent that, if, beloved
Geraldine, you will agree to adopt it.'

'Yes.'

'By becoming *my* wife at once. We would return to
London as soon as the ceremony was over; and there
you may defy them all.'

'Oh, Egbert I have thought of this—'

'You will have no reason to regret it. Perhaps I
can introduce you to as intellectual, if odd-mannered
and less aristocratic society than that you have been
accustomed to.'

'Yes, I know it—I reflected on it before I came . . .
I will be your wife,' she replied tenderly. 'I have come
to you, and to you I will cling.'

Egbert kissed her lips then for the first time in his
life. He reflected for some time, if that process could
be called reflection which was accompanied with so
much excitement.

'The parson of your parish would perhaps refuse to

marry us, even if we could get to the church secretly,' he said, with a cloud on his brow. ' That's a difficulty.'

' Oh, don't take me there! I cannot go to Tollamore. I shall be seen, or we shall be parted. Don't take me there.'

' No, no; I will not, love; I was only thinking. Are you known in this parish?'

' Well, yes; not, however, to the clergyman. He is a young man—old Mr. Keene is dead, you know.'

' Then I can manage it.' Egbert clasped her in his arms in the delight of his heart. ' Now this is our course. I am first going to the surrogate's, and then further; and while I am gone you must stay in this house absolutely alone, and lock yourself in for safety. There is food in the house, and wine in that cupboard; you must stay here in hiding until I come back. It is now five o'clock. I will be here again at latest by eleven. If anybody knocks, remain silent, and the house will be supposed empty, as it lately has been so for a long time. My old servant and waitress must not come here today—I will manage that. I will light a fire, which will have burnt down by daylight, so that the room will be warmed for you. Sit there while I set about it.'

He lit the fire, placed on the table all the food the house afforded, and went away.

## CHAPTER 6

Hence will I to my ghostly father's cell;
His help to crave, and my dear hap to tell.[33]

In half an hour Egbert returned, leading a horse.

'I have borrowed this from an old neighbour,' he said, 'and I have told the woman that waits upon me that I am going on a journey, and shall lock up the house today, so that she will not be wanted. And now, dearest, I want you to lend me something.'

'Whatever it may be, you know it is yours.'

'It is that ,' he answered, lightly touching with the tip of his finger a sparkling ring that she wore on hers—the same she had used to wear at their youthful meetings in past years. 'I want it as a pattern for the size.'

She drew it off and handed it to him, at the same time raising her eyelids and glancing under his with a little laugh of confusion. His heart responded, and he kissed her; but he could not help feeling that she was by far too fair a prize for him.

She accompanied him to the door, and Mayne mounted the horse. They parted, and, waiting to hear

[33] Quoted from Shakespeare's *Romeo and Juliet* (II, ii, 189). See notes 2 (p. 21), 26 (p. 89), and 32 (p. 114). For further evidence of Hardy's extensive indebtedness to Shakespeare, see Carl J. Weber, "Twin Voice of Shakespeare," *Shakespeare Association Bulletin* (9: 91-97, 162-163), April and July, 1934.

her lock herself in, he cantered off by a bridle-path towards a town about five miles off.[34]

It was so early that the surrogate on whom he called had not yet breakfasted, but he was very willing to see Mayne, and took him at once to the study. Egbert briefly told him what he wanted; that the lady he wished to marry was at that very moment in his house, and could go nowhere else for shelter — hence the earliness and urgency of his errand.

The surrogate seemed to see rather less interest in the circumstances than Mayne did himself; but he at once prepared the application for a license. When it was done, he made it up into a letter, directed it, and placed it on the mantlepiece. 'It shall go by this evening's post,' he said.

'But, ' said Egbert, 'considering the awkward position this lady is in, cannot a special messenger be sent for the license? It is only seven or eight miles to —, and yet otherwise I must wait for two days' posts.'

'Undoubtedly; if anybody likes to pay for it, a special messenger may be sent.'

'There will be no paying; I am willing to go myself. Do you object?'

---

[34] Puddletown is five miles distant, but Hardy purposely leaves the town unnamed, in order to facilitate the geographical telescoping explained in note 35. See map, p. 85.

' No; if the case is really serious, and the lady is dangerously compromised by every delay.'

Mayne left the vicarage of the surrogate and again rode off; this time it was towards a well-known cathedral town.[35] He felt bewildering sensations during this stroke for happiness, and went on his journey in that state of mind which takes cognisance of little things, without at the time being conscious of them, though they return vividly upon the memory long after.

He reached the city after a ride of seven additional miles, and soon obtained the precious document, and all else that he required. Returning to the inn where the horse had been rested, rubbed down, and fed, he again crossed the saddle, and at ten minutes past eleven he was back at Fairland. Before going to Monk's Hut, where Geraldine was immured, he hastened straight to the parsonage.

The young clergyman looked curiously at him and at

[35] The " well-known cathedral town " is Salisbury, which figures in many of Hardy's novels. It is actually many more than " seven or eight miles " away; but Hardy was here doing what, by his own confession, he did also in *Far From the Madding Crowd* and in *Two on a Tower:* he was performing some topographical squeezing, in order to make it possible for Mayne to accomplish his ride in the time allowed. When there was no reason for concealment of the actual distance, " Melchester " was described by Hardy in sufficient detail to identify it, in site and features, as Salisbury. Hardy's " Melchester " was Trollope's " Barchester." For a study of Trollope's influence on Hardy, see Carl J. Weber, *In Thomas Hardy's Workshop*, Colby College Monographs No. 6, Waterville (Maine), 1934.

the bespattered and jaded horse outside. ' Surely you are too rash in the matter,' he said.

' No,' said Egbert; ' there are weighty reasons why I should be in such haste. The lady has at present no home to go to. She has taken shelter with me. I am doing what I consider best in so awkward a case.'

The parson took down his hat, and said, ' Very well; I will go to the church at once. You must be quick if it is to be done today.'

Mayne left the horse for the present in the parson's yard, ran round to the clerk, thence to Monk's Hut, and called Geraldine.

It was, indeed, a hasty preparation for a wedding ceremony that these two made that morning. She was standing at the window, quite ready, and feverish with waiting. Kissing her gaily and breathlessly he directed her by a slightly circuitous path to the church; and, when she had gone about two minutes, proceeded thither himself by the direct road, so that they met in the porch. Within, the clergyman, clerk, and clerk's wife had already gathered; and Geraldine and Egbert advanced to the communion railing.

Thus they became man and wife.

' Now he cannot claim me anyhow,' she murmured when the service was ended, as she sank almost fainting upon the arm of Mayne.

' Mr. Mayne,' said the clergyman, aside to him in

the vestry, ' what is the name of the family at Tollamore House? '

' Strangely enough, Allenville—the same as hers,' said he, coolly.

The parson looked keenly and dubiously at Mayne, and Egbert returned the look, whereupon the other turned aside and said nothing.

Egbert and Geraldine returned to their hermitage on foot, as they had left it; and, by rigorously excluding all thoughts of the future, they felt happy with the same old unreasoning happiness as of six years before, now resumed for the first time since that date.

But it was quite impossible that the hastily-married pair should remain at Monk's Hut unseen and unknown, as they fain would have done. Almost as soon as they had sat down in the house they came to the conclusion that there was no alternative for them but to start at once for Melport, if not for London. The difficulty was to get a conveyance. The only horse obtainable here, though a strong one, had already been tired down by Egbert in the morning, and the nearest village at which another could be had was about two miles off.

' I can walk as far as that,' said Geraldine.

' Then walk we will,' said Egbert. ' It will remove all our difficulty.' And, first packing up a small valise, he locked the door and went off with her upon his arm, just as the church clock struck one.

That walk through the woods was as romantic an experience as any they had ever known in their lives, though Geraldine was far from being quite happy. On reaching the village, which was larger than Fairland, they were fortunate enough to secure a carriage without any trouble. The village stood on the turnpike road, and a fly, about to return to Melport, where it had come from, was halting before the inn. Egbert hired it at once, and in little less than an hour and a half bridegroom and bride were comfortably housed in a quiet hotel of the seaport town above mentioned.

## CHAPTER 7

How small a part of time they share
That are so wondrous sweet and fair! [36]

They remained three days at Melport without having come to any decision on their future movements.

On the third day, at breakfast, Egbert took up the local newspaper which had been published that morning, and his eye presently glanced upon a paragraph headed ' The Tollamore Elopement.'

Before reading it he considered for a moment whether he should lay the journal aside, and for the present hide its contents from the tremulous creature opposite. But deeming this unadvisable, he gently prepared her for the news, and read the paragraph aloud.

It was to the effect that the village of Tollamore and its neighbourhood had been thrown into an unwonted state of excitement by the disappearance of Miss Allenville on the eve of the preparations for her marriage with Lord Bretton, which had been alluded to in their last number. Simultaneously there had disappeared from a neighbouring village, whither he had come for a few months' retirement, a gentleman named Mayne, of considerable literary reputation in the metropolis,

---

[36] Quoted from Edmund Waller's " Go, Lovely Rose," 19-20. See *The Golden Treasury*, CXV (p. 91, ed. 1906, Macmillan). — Other unidentified quotations appearing in this story have eluded all editorial efforts.

and apparently an old acquaintance of Miss Allenville's. Efforts had been made to trace the fugitives by the young lady's father and the distracted bridegroom, Lord Bretton, but hitherto all their exertions had been unvailing.

Subjoined was another paragraph, entitled ' Latest particulars.'

' It has just been discovered that Mr. Mayne and Miss Allenville are already man and wife. They were boldly married at the parish church of Fairland, before any person in the village had the least suspicion who or what they were. It appears that the lady joined her intended husband early that morning at the cottage he had taken for the season, that they went to the church by different paths, and after the ceremony walked out of the parish by a route as yet unknown. In consequence of this intelligence Lord Bretton has returned to London, and her father is left alone to mourn the young lady's rashness.'

Egbert lifted his eyes and watched Geraldine as he finished reading. On perceiving his look she tried to smile. The smile thinned away, for there was not cheerfulness enough to support it long, and she said faintly, ' Egbert, what must be done? '

' We must, I suppose, leave this place, darling; as charming as our life is here.'

' Yes; I fear we must.'

' London seems to be the spot for us at once, before we attract the attention of people here.'

'How well everything might end,' she said, 'if my father were induced to welcome you, and make the most of your reputation! I wonder, wonder if he would! In that case there would be little amiss.'

Mayne, after some reflection, said, 'I think that I will go to your father before we leave for town. We are certain to be discovered by somebody or other, either here or in London, and that would bring your father, and there would possibly result a public meeting between him and myself at which words might be uttered which could not be forgotten on either side; so that a private meeting and explanation is safest, before anything of that sort can happen.'

'I think,' she said, looking to see if he approved of her words as they fell, 'I think that a still better course would be for me to go to him—alone.'

Mayne did not care much about this plan at first; but further discussion gave it a more feasible aspect, since Allenville, though stern and proud, was fond of his daughter, and had never crossed her, except when her whims interfered, as he considered, with her interests. Nothing could unmarry them; and Geraldine's mind would be much more at ease after begging her father's forgiveness. The journey was therefore decided on. They waited till nearly evening, and then, ordering round a brougham, Egbert told the man to drive to Tollamore.

The journey to Geraldine was tedious and oppressive to a degree. When, after two hours' driving, they drew near the park precincts, she said shivering,

' I don't like to drive up to the house, Egbert.'

' I will do just as you like. What do you propose? '

' To let him wait in the road, under the three oak trees, while you and I walk to the house.'

Egbert humoured her in everything; and when they reached the designated spot the driver was stopped, and they alighted. Carefully wrapping her up he gave her his arm, and they started for Tollamore House at an easy pace through the moonlit park, avoiding the direct road as much as possible.

Geraldine spoke but little during the walk, especially when they neared the house, and passed across the smooth broad glade which surrounded it. At sight of the door she seemed to droop, and leant heavy upon him. Egbert more than ever wished to confront Mr. Allenville himself; morally and socially it appeared to him the right thing to do. But Geraldine trembled when he again proposed it; and he yielded to her entreaty thus far, that he would wait a few minutes till she had entered and seen her father privately, and prepared the way for Egbert to follow, which he would then do in due course.

The spot in which she desired him to wait was a summer-house under a tree about fifty yards from the

lawn front of the house, and commanding a view of the door on this side. She was to enter unobserved by the servants, and go straight to her father, when, should he listen to her with the least show of mildness, she would send out for Egbert to follow. If the worst were to happen, and he were to be enraged with her, refusing to listen to entreaties or explanations, she would hasten out, rejoin Egbert, and depart.

In this little summer-house he embraced her, and bade her adieu, after their honeymoon of three short days. She trembled so much that she could scarcely walk when he let go her hand.

' Don't go alone—you are not well,' said Egbert.

' Yes, yes, dearest, I am—and I will soon return, so soon! ' she answered; and he watched her crossing the grass and advancing, a mere dot, towards the mansion. In a short time the appearance of an oblong of light in the shadowy expanse of wall denoted to him that the door was open: her outline appeared on it; then the door shut her in, and all was shadow as before. Even though they were husband and wife the line of demarcation seemed to be drawn again as rigidly as when he lived at the school.

Egbert waited in the solitude of this place minute by minute, restlessly swinging his foot when seated, at other times walking up and down, and anxiously watch-

ing for the arrival of some messenger. Nearly half an
hour passed, but no messenger came.

The first sign of life in the neighbourhood of the
house was in the shape of a man on horseback, gallop-
ing from the stable entrance. Egbert saw this by looking over the wall at the back of the summer-house; and
the man passed along the open drive, vanishing in the
direction of the lodge. Mayne, not without some pre-
sentiment of ill, wondered what it could mean, but
thought it just possible that the horseman was a special
messenger sent to catch the late post at the nearest
town, as was sometimes done by Squire Allenville. So
he curbed his impatience for Geraldine's sake.

Next he observed lights moving in the upper windows
of the building. ' It has been made known to them all
that she is come, and they are preparing a room,' he
thought hopefully.

But nobody came from the door to welcome him;
his existence was apparently forgotten by the whole
world. In another ten minutes he saw the Melport
brougham that had brought them, creeping slowly up
to the house. Egbert went round to the man, and told
him to drive to the stables and wait for orders.

From the length of Geraldine's absence, Mayne could
not help concluding that the impression produced on
her father was of a doubtful kind, not quite favorable

enough to warrant her in telling him at once that her husband was in waiting. Still, a sense of his dignity as her husband might have constrained her to introduce him as soon as possible, and he had only agreed to wait a few minutes. Something unexpected must, after all, have occurred. And this supposition was confirmed a moment later by the noise of a horse and carriage coming up the drive. Egbert again looked over into the open park, and saw the vehicle reach the carriage entrance, where somebody alighted and went in.

'Her father away from home perhaps, and now just returned,' he said.

He lingered yet another ten minutes, and then could endure no longer. Before he could reach the lawn door through which Geraldine had disappeared, it opened. A person came out and, without shutting the door, hastened across to where Egbert stood. The man was a servant, without a hat on, and the moment that he saw Mayne he ran up to him.

'Mr. Mayne?' he said.

'It is,' said Egbert.

'Mr. Allenville desires that you will come with me. There is something serious the matter. Miss Allenville is taken dangerously ill, and she wishes to see you.'

'What has happened to her?' gasped Egbert breathlessly.

'Miss Allenville came unexpectedly home just now,

and directly she saw her father it gave her such a turn that she fainted, and ruptured a blood-vessel internally, and fell upon the floor. They have put her to bed, and the doctor has come, but we are afraid she won't live over it. She has suffered from it before.' [37]

Egbert did not speak, but walked hastily beside the man-servant. The only recollection that he ever had in after years of entering that house was a vague idea of stags' antlers in a long row on the wall, and a sense of great breadth in the stone staircase as he ascended it. Everything else was in a mist.

Mr. Allenville, on being informed of his arrival, came out and met him in the corridor.

Egbert's mind was so entirely given up to the one thought that the life of his Geraldine was in danger, that he quite forgot the peculiar circumstances under which he met Allenville, and the peculiar behaviour necessary on that account. He seized her father's hand, and said abruptly,

' Where is she? Is the danger great?'

Allenville withdrew his hand, turned, and led the way into his daughter's room, merely saying in a low hard tone, ' Your wife is in great danger, sir.'

---

[37] Hardy *may* have been writing here from personal experience. Whether he, like Geraldine, had " suffered from it before " is not known; but two years after the publication of these words he, like Miss Allenville, had an internal hemorrhage which " put him to bed " for nearly six months.

Egbert rushed to the bedside and bent over her in agony not to be described. Allenville sent the attendants from the room, and closed the door.

'Father,' she whispered feebly, 'I cannot help loving him. Would you leave us alone? We are very dear to each other, and perhaps I shall soon die.'

'Anything you wish, child,' he said with stern anguish; 'and anything can hardly include more.' Seeing that she looked hurt at this, he spoke more pleasantly. 'I am glad to please you—you know I am, Geraldine—to the utmost.' He then went out.

'They would not have let you know if Dr. Williams had not insisted,' she said. 'I could not speak to explain at first—that's how it is you have been left there so long.'

'Geraldine, dear, dear Geraldine, why should all this have come upon us?' he said in unbroken accents.

'Perhaps it is best,' she murmured. 'I hardly knew what I was doing when I entered the door, or how I could explain to my father, or what could be done to reconcile him to us. He kept me waiting a little time before he would see me, but at last he came into the room. I felt a fulness on my chest, I could not speak, and then this happened to me. Papa has asked no questions.'

A silence followed, interrupted only by her fitful breathing:

A silence which doth follow talk, that causes
The baffled heart to speak with sighs and tears.

'Do you love me very much now, Egbert?' she said.
'After all my vacillation, do you?'

'Yes—how can you doubt?'

'I do not doubt. I know you love me. But will you
stay here till I get better? You must stay. Papa is
sure to be friendly with you now.'

'Don't agitate yourself, dearest, about me. All is
right with me here. Your health is the one thing to
be anxious about now.'

'I have only been taken ill like this once before in
my life, and I thought it would never be again.'

As she was not allowed to speak much, he remained
holding her hand; and after some time she sank into
a light sleep. Egbert then went from the chamber for
a moment, and asked the physician, who was in the next
room, if there was good hope for her life.

'It is a dangerous attack, and she is very weak,' he
replied, concealing, though scarcely able to conceal,
the curiosity with which he regarded Egbert; for the
marriage had now become generally known.

The evening and night wore on. Great events in
which he could not participate seemed to be passing
over Egbert's head; a stir was in progress, of whose
results he grasped but small and fragmentary notions.
And, on the other hand, it was mournfully strange to

141

notice her father's behaviour during these hours of doubt. It was only when he despaired that he looked upon Egbert with tolerance. When he hoped, the young man's presence was hateful to him.

Not knowing what to do when out of her chamber, having nobody near him to whom he could speak on intimate terms, Egbert passed a wretched time of three long days. After watching by her for several hours on the third day, he went downstairs, and into the open air. There intelligence was brought him that another effusion, more violent than any which preceded it, had taken place. Egbert rushed back to her room. Powerful remedies were applied, but none availed. A fainting-fit followed, and in two or three hours it became plain to those who understood that there was no Geraldine for the morrow.

Sometimes she was lethargic, and as if her spirit had already flown; then her mind wandered; but towards the end she was sensible of all that was going on, though unable to speak, her strength being barely enough to enable her to receive an idea.

It was a gentle death. She was as acquiescent as if she had been a saint, which was not the least striking and uncommon feature in the life of this fair and unfortunate lady. Her husband held one tiny hand, remaining all the time on the right side of the bed in a nook beside the curtains, while her father and the rest

remained on the left side, never raising their eyes to him, and scarcely ever addressing him.

Everything was so still that her weak act of trying to live seemed a silent wrestling with all the powers of the universe. Pale and hopelessly anxious they all waited and watched the heavy shadows close over her. It might have been thought that death felt for her and took her tenderly. She sighed twice or three times; then her heart stood still; and this strange family alliance was at an end for ever.

THOMAS HARDY

No one who has qualified for a reading of this story, by forming a previous acquaintance with a half dozen or so of the Wessex Novels, will stand in any need of critical comment on this early composition. It is stamped throughout with the genuine Hardy marks, good and bad; and even without his name attached to it, one might have been sure of the authorship.

Any reader who may *not* have acquired such previous qualification for judging will perhaps be interested in this summarizing list of a dozen typical Hardy features found in *An Indiscretion*:

1. Its stage is chiefly set in rural Wessex.

2. It is topographically specific, to a degree unparalleled in English literature.

3. It deals with Dorset farmers, and shows sympathetic insight into the life of this class.

4. It does not avoid an impression of artificiality whenever " polite society " is involved.

5. The dialogue is often unreal, and there is occasional stiffness of language, with involved sentences, awkward inversions, split infinitives, etc.

6. In marked contrast with these rhetorical defects, there is frequent felicity of phrase, particularly in descriptive passages; and the author's alert senses, all of them, often leave their mark.

7. Nature interests him for her own sake, and his treatment of her is often poetic.

8. There are many literary allusions and quotations, and references to painters, musicians, and architects.

9. The use of coincidents and accidents is overdone, and plausibilty is often stretched to the extreme.

10. There is a secret marriage.

11. There is a pervading note of gloom, only momentarily relieved.

12. It all comes to a tragic end.

All these elements, discernible in 1868, are identical with those shown in the literary product of the next twenty-five years. This first novel shows us how truly the Child was Father of the Man.

C. J. W.